U0079384

英文 ENGLISH
GRAMMAR 文法

不小心就 學會了

前言

　　看過很多坊間的英文文法書，也因為教學的關係用過很多英文文法書，發現大多數都是一本書講文法講到底，類似一條條的數學公式給你，然後你要一條條的去吸收、去記憶，能不能消化是另外一回事了。薄一點的也許還可以勉強讀完，厚一點深一點的，這麼多年的教學經驗告訴我，通常到最後只是用了前面的幾章，而如果沒有人教、沒有人引導，自己要去啃一本又厚又深的文法書，不是覺得太無聊而讀不下去，就是覺得無法吸收而打退堂鼓了。

　　因此我一直在想，怎麼樣可以讓一本文法書讓初學者讀起來不覺得無聊，也不覺得吃力，而且不會像是大部分的文法書那樣，一個公式給你，然後底下一堆題目，感覺好像在算數學一樣。畢竟語言可以傳遞的東西太多了，你可以在語言裡讀到文化、歷史、資訊、生活等等各種的訊息，你可以在理性的文字裡潛移默化得到感動，這些都是學習語言無形的樂趣跟收穫，於是，從這樣面向出發，我想編寫一本英文文法書是可以讓初學者在面對理性為主的文法時，也同時能透過完整的文字篇章，並在專業外籍教師聲音的引導及輔助下，觸覺到英文的感性，也許這樣學起文法會更有趣而且輕鬆的多了吧。

　　於是，這本易於攜帶、簡單輕鬆的英文文法書，在講解每

一個文法時，都會搭配一篇該文法出現很多次的小短文或是小段落，這些小短文或是小段落也都會有外籍老師錄音，並有中文翻譯及重點解說，讓你學文法不再只是學文法，而是從一個帶有精神內容的短文或段落下去學文法，這樣就會學得更豐富更活用，可以在一個實際的範例下看到文法的運用，同時也學到單字、片語、句子，甚至於整篇文章或整個段落的文化精神等等其他比較偏向無形及感性的學習。

由於在每個文法單元最後也會附上與範例文章或段落相關的練習題，所以可說是一本涵蓋了聽、說、讀、寫的全方位英文文法書。相信這樣的一本文法書，因為其融合而多元，讓你讀起來可能也會忘了這是一本文法書，你的英文文法，可能就在這樣的簡單、輕鬆、豐富的情境下，「不小心」就學會了吧，親愛的讀者們您說您豈能不試試呢！

英文文法 ㊉㊒學會了

目錄

附錄、重要動詞的用法

主詞和be動詞

重點一

主詞跟be動詞的搭配

一、be動詞的現在式

am、is、are，中文表「是」。

二、be動詞需與主詞搭配

(1) 第一人稱

| 第一人稱單數「我」 | I + am |
| 第一人稱複數「我們」 | we + are |

(2) 第二人稱

| 第二人稱單數「你」 | you + are |
| 第二人稱複數「你們」 | you + are |

(3) 第三人稱

| 第三人稱單數「他、她、它」 | he / she / it + is |
| 第三人稱複數「他們、她們、它們」 | they + are |

(4) 複數主詞

如「students, John and Mary, teachers...」：

☞ students (學生們) + are...

☞ John and Mary (約翰和瑪莉) + are...

☞ teachers (老師們) + are...

(5) 單數主詞

如「a student, John, Mary, the teacher...」：

☞ a student (一個學生) + is...

☞ John (約翰) + is...

☞ Mary (瑪莉) + is...

☞ the teacher (這個老師) + is...

Track 001

My Family

I am Vicky. I have a happy family. My father is a teacher and my mother is a secretary. They are busy every day. I have two brothers and one sister. My older brother is a salesman. Both my younger brother and sister are students. They like to study together. They are just like good friends. I am a student, too. Because I like animals, we have three dogs. They are my good friends. We are happy every day.

我的家庭

我是維琪。我有一個快樂的家庭。我爸爸是一個老師，而我媽媽是一個祕書。他們每天都很忙碌。我有兩個兄弟跟一個妹妹。我哥哥是一個業務員。我弟弟跟我妹妹兩個都是學生。他們喜歡一起念書。他們就像好朋友一樣。我也是一個學生。因為我喜歡動物，我們養了三隻狗。它們是我的好朋友。我們每天都很快樂。

1. happy【ˋhæpɪ】 形容詞 快樂的

2. family【ˋfæməlɪ】 名詞 家庭，家人

3. father【ˋfɑðɚ】 名詞 父親，爸爸

4. teacher【ˋtitʃɚ】 名詞 老師

5. mother【ˋmʌðɚ】 名詞 母親，媽媽

6. secretary【ˋsɛkrəˏtɛrɪ】 名詞 祕書

7. busy【ˋbɪzɪ】 形容詞 忙碌的

8. every day【ˋɛvrɪde】 副詞片語 每天

9. brother【ˋbrʌðɚ】 名詞 兄弟；兄，弟

10. sister【ˋsɪstɚ】 名詞 姐妹；姐姐，妹妹

11. older【ˋoldɚ】 形容詞比較級 較老的，年紀較大的

12. salesman【ˋselzmən】 名詞 推銷員，業務員

13. both + A + and + B　A跟B兩者皆…

14. younger【ˋjʌŋgɚ】 形容詞比較級 較年輕的，年紀較小的

15. student【ˋstjudn̩t】 名詞 學生

16. like【laɪk】（like + to V / V-ing） 動詞 喜歡

17. study【ˋstʌdɪ】 動詞 學習，用功

18. together【təˋgɛðɚ】 副詞 一起，共同

19. just【dʒʌst】 副詞 正好，就是

20. like【laɪk】 介係詞 像

21. too【tu】 副詞 也

22. animal【ˋænəml̩】 名詞 動物

23. have【hæv】動詞 有

24. dog【dɔg】名詞 狗

25. friend【frɛnd】名詞 朋友

練習題

I. 填入適當的be動詞

1. It _____ a good idea.

2. Kelly _____ very cute.

3. Those dogs _____ fierce(兇猛的).

4. The teacher _____ serious(嚴格的).

5. You _____ my good friend.

6. These books _____ interesting(有趣的).

7. Luna and Kelly _____ my good friends.

8. He _____ lazy(懶惰的).

9. She _____ very beautiful(美麗的).

10. The weather(天氣)_____ cold(寒冷的) today.

II. 請找出《實際運用短文 - My Family》一文中有運用
　　到「主詞＋be動詞」的句子，請將「主詞＋be動詞」
　　劃上底線。

解答 ....

I.

1	is	2	is	3	are	4	is	5	are
6	are	7	are	8	is	9	is	10	is

II.

1. <u>I am</u> Vicky.

2. <u>My father is</u> a teacher and <u>my mother is</u> a secretary.

3. <u>They are</u> busy every day.

4. <u>My older brother is</u> a salesman.

5. <u>Both my younger brother and sister are</u> students.

6. <u>They are</u> just like good friends.

7. <u>I am</u> a student, too.

8. <u>They are</u> my good friends.

9. <u>We are</u> happy every day.

重點二

be動詞的否定句

Part
1

一、

be動詞 + not = 否定句 =「不是」

二、

is not	可縮寫成 isn't【`ɪzənt】
are not	可縮寫成 aren't【ɑrnt】
am not	不能縮寫

例句1：He isn't my classmate.

　　　　他不是我同學。

例句2：We are not basketball players.

　　　　我們不是籃球員。

例句3：I am not tall.

　　　　我不高。

John and Mark

John and Mark are not brothers. They are not good friends, either. They have different hobbies. John likes to read books. He is not good at sports. Mark likes to play basketball. He is good at sports. However, they are classmates. I am their good friend, but I am not their classmate.

約翰和馬克

約翰和馬克不是兄弟。他們也不是好朋友。他們有不同的嗜好。約翰喜歡閱讀書籍,不擅長於運動。馬克喜歡打籃球,擅長於運動。不過他們是同班同學。我是他們的好朋友,但我不是他們的同班同學。

重點註解 ➡ Track 002

1. either【`iðɚ】 副詞 也（用在否定句中）

2. different【`dɪfərənt】 形容詞 不同的

3. hobby【`hɑbɪ】 名詞 嗜好

4. read【rid】 動詞 讀

5. book【bʊk】 名詞 書

6. be good at　擅長於⋯

7. sports【sport】 名詞 運動

8. play＋球類　打⋯球

9. basketball【`bæskɪt,bɔl】 名詞 籃球

10. however【haʊ`ɛvɚ】 副詞 然而，不過

11. classmate【`klæs,met】 名詞 同班同學

12. but【bʌt】 對等連接詞 但是

練習題

I. 填入適當的be動詞否定式

1. Kelly ＿＿＿＿ ＿＿＿＿ a student.

2. Lisa and Helen ＿＿＿＿ ＿＿＿＿ classmates.

3. It ＿＿＿＿ ＿＿＿＿ an interesting(有趣的) book.

4. I ＿＿＿ ＿＿＿ happy today.

5. Kaohsiung ＿＿＿＿ ＿＿＿＿ a small(小的) city(城市).

6. The weather(天氣)＿＿＿＿ ＿＿＿＿ fine(好的) today.

7. They _____ _____ good friends.

8. You _____ _____ tall (高的).

9. My father _____ _____ a teacher.

10. The students _____ _____ in the classroom (教室).

II. 請找出《實際運用短文 - John and Mark》一文中有運
用到「be動詞 + not」的否定句，並將「be動詞 + not」
劃上底線。

解答

I.

1	is not	2	are not
3	is not	4	am not
5	is not	6	is not
7	are not	8	are not
9	is not	10	are not

II.

1. John and Mark <u>are not</u> brothers.

2. They <u>are not</u> good friends, either.

3. He <u>is not</u> good at sports.

4. I am their good friends, but I <u>am not</u> their classmates.

英文文法 秒學會了   25

重點三

be動詞的疑問句

一、

將「主詞＋be動詞」改為「be動詞＋主詞…？」
要記得將句尾改成問號「？」

例句1：Her father is a teacher.

(肯定句) 她父親是老師。

→ Is her father a teacher？

(疑問句) 她父親是老師嗎？

例句2：She is your classmate.

(肯定句) 她是你的同學。

→ Is she your classmate？

(疑問句) 她是你的同學嗎？

例句3：You are his good friend.

(肯定句) 你是他的好朋友。

→ Are you his good friend？

(疑問句) 你是他的好朋友嗎？

二、回答時，可用簡答或詳答的方式：

(1)

肯定簡答	Yes, 代名詞 + be動詞.
肯定詳答	Yes, (代名詞 + be動詞.) + 句子.

例句1：Is her father a teacher?
　　　　她父親是老師嗎？

簡答 Yes, he is.
　　　是的，他是。

詳答 Yes, he is. He is a teacher.
　　　是的，他是。他是老師。

詳答 Yes, he is a teacher.
　　　是的，他是老師。

例句2：Is she your classmate?
　　　　她是你的同學嗎？

簡答 Yes, she is.
　　　是的，她是。

詳答 Yes, she is. She is my classmate.
　　　是的，她是。她是我同學。

詳答 Yes, she is my classmate.
　　　是的，她是我同學。

例句3：Are you his good friend?

　　　　你是他的好朋友嗎？

簡答　Yes, I am.

　　　是的，我是。

詳答　Yes, I am. I am his good friend.

　　　是的，我是。我是他的好朋友。

詳答　Yes, I am his good friend.

　　　是的，我是他的好朋友。

(2)

否定簡答	No, 代名詞＋be動詞＋not (可用縮寫體).
否定詳答	No,〔代名詞＋be動詞＋not (可用縮寫體).〕＋否定句子.

例句1：Is her father a teacher?

　　　　她父親是老師嗎？

簡答　No, he is not. (或 No, he isn't.)

　　　不，他不是。

詳答　No, he is not.(或 No, he isn't.) He is not a teacher.

　　　不，他不是。他不是老師。

詳答　No, he is not(或 isn't) a teacher.

　　　不，他不是老師。

例句2：Is she your classmate?

　　　她是你的同學嗎？

簡答 No, she is not.（或 No, she isn't.）

　　　不，她不是。

詳答 No, she is not.（或 No, she isn't.）She is not my

　　　classmate.

　　　不，她不是。她不是我同學。

詳答 No, she is not（或 isn't）my classmate.

　　　不，她不是我同學。

例句3：Are you his good friend?

　　　你是他的好朋友嗎？

簡答 No, I am not.

　　　不，我不是。

詳答 No, I am not. I am not his good friend.

　　　不，我不是。我不是他的好朋友。

詳答 No, I am not his good friend.

　　　不，我不是他的好朋友。

What is A Good Student?

What is a good student? Are you a good student? Am I a good student? Is John a good student? Are my sisters good students? Are my friends good students?

Is a good student smart? Is a bad student stupid? Is a good student hard-working? Is a bad student lazy? Is a good student always on time? Is a bad student often late?

什麼是好學生？

什麼是好學生？你是好學生嗎？我是好學生嗎？約翰是好學生嗎？我姐妹是好學生嗎？我朋友們是好學生嗎？

好學生聰明嗎？壞學生笨嗎？好學生努力嗎？壞學生懶惰嗎？好學生總是準時嗎？壞學生常常遲到嗎？

重點註解 Track 003

1. what 【hwɑt】 疑問詞 什麼
2. good 【gʊd】 形容詞 好的
3. student 【ˋstjudn̩t】 名詞 學生
4. smart 【smɑrt】 形容詞 聰明的
5. bad 【bæd】 形容詞 壞的

6. stupid 【`stjupɪd】 形容詞 笨的

7. hard-working 【ˌhɑrd`wɝkɪŋ】 形容詞 努力的

8. lazy 【`lezɪ】 形容詞 懶惰的

9. always 【`ɔlwez】 副詞 總是

10. on time 【ɑn】【taɪm】 介系詞片語 準時

11. often 【`ɔfən】 副詞 常常

12. late 【let】 形容詞 遲的

練習題

I. 將下列句子改為疑問句

1. My father is a good cook(廚師).

2. Those dogs are cute.

3. Mary is a dancer(舞者).

4. They are good friends.

5. The cat is on the grass(草地).

II. 請找出《實際運用短文 - What is A Good Student?》一文中有運用到「be動詞＋主詞…?」的疑問句，並將「be動詞＋主詞」劃上底線。

解答

I.

1	Is my father a good cook?
2	Are those dogs cute?
3	Is Mary a dancer?
4	Are they good friends?
5	Is the cat on the grass?

II.

1. <u>Are you</u> a good student?

2. <u>Am I</u> a good student?

3. <u>Is John</u> a good student?

4. <u>Are my sisters</u> good students?

5. <u>Are my friends</u> good students?

6. <u>Is a good student</u> smart?

7. <u>Is a bad student</u> stupid?

8. <u>Is a good student</u> hard-working?

9. <u>Is a bad student</u> lazy?

10. <u>Is a good student</u> always on time?

11. <u>Is a bad student</u> often late?

主格、所有格、
受格

重點一

單數人稱的主格、所有格、受格

單數人稱

	主格		所有格		受格	
第一人稱	I	我	my	我的	me	我
第二人稱	you	你	your	你的	you	你
第三人稱	he	他	his	他的	him	他
	she	她	her	她的	her	她
	it	它	its	它的	it	它

重點二

複數人稱的主格、所有格、受格

複數人稱

	主格		所有格		受格	
第一人稱	we	我們	our	我們的	us	我們
第二人稱	you	你們	your	你們的	you	你們
第三人稱	they	他們 她們 它們	their	他們的 她們的 它們的	them	他們 她們 它們

用法説明

(1)

主格當主詞用	主格 + be動詞
	主格 + 一般動詞

例句1： <u>I am</u> a student.

我是個學生。

例句2： <u>We are</u> classmates.

我們是同學。

例句3： <u>They like</u> to sing.

他們喜歡唱歌。

例句4： <u>You sing</u> well.

你很會唱歌。

(2)

所有格 + 名詞

例句1： <u>My dog</u> is cute.

我的狗很可愛。

例句2： <u>Her boyfriend</u> is handsome.

她男朋友很帥。

例句3： <u>Your watch</u> is expensive.

你的手錶很貴。

例句4：<u>Their cats</u> are on the grass.

他們的貓在草地上。

(3)

受格當受詞用	動詞 + 受格
	介係詞 + 受格

例句1：I <u>like her</u>.

我喜歡她。

例句2：Mary <u>hates them</u>.

瑪莉討厭他們。

例句3：He wants to talk <u>to us</u>.

他想跟我們說話。

例句4：She likes to play <u>with me</u>.

她喜歡跟我一起玩耍。

實際運用短文 ⟶ Track 004

A DVD Movie

David has a DVD movie. The movie is about a farmer and his neighbor. The farmer has three dogs. He likes his dogs a lot. But his neighbor doesn't like them, because they bark at him every day. I like this movie, because I think it is interesting.

一部DVD電影

　　大衛有一部DVD電影。那部電影是有關一個農夫跟他的鄰居。農夫有三隻狗。他很喜歡他的狗。但是他的鄰居不喜歡牠們，因為牠們每天都對他吠叫。我喜歡這部電影，因為我覺得它有趣。

重點註解 ⟶ Track 004

1. movie【ˋmuvɪ】 名詞 電影
2. about【əˋbaʊt】 介係詞 關於
3. farmer【ˋfɑrmɚ】 名詞 農夫
4. neighbor【ˋnebɚ】 名詞 鄰居
5. dog【dɔg】 名詞 狗
6. like【laɪk】 動詞 喜歡
7. a lot【ə】【lɑt】 副詞片語 非常，很⋯
8. doesn't + 原形動詞 為「否定句型」，表「不⋯」
9. because【bɪˋkɔz】 (副詞連接詞)因為
10. bark【bɑrk】 + at【æt】(介係詞) + 人 表「對⋯人吠叫」
11. think【θɪŋk】 動詞 想，認為
12. interesting【ˋɪntərɪstɪŋ】 形容詞 有趣的

I. 請找出《實際運用短文 - A DVD Movie》一文中有運
　 用到「主格當主詞用:『主格＋be動詞』或『主格＋
　 一般動詞』」的句子,並將『主格＋be動詞』或『主
　 格＋一般動詞』的部分劃上底線。

II. 請找出《實際運用短文 - A DVD Movie》一文中有運
　　用到「所有格＋名詞」的句子,並將「所有格＋名詞」
　　的部分劃上底線。

III. 請找出《實際運用短文 - A DVD Movie》一文中有
　　 運用到「受格當受詞用:『動詞＋受格』或『介係
　　 詞＋受格』」的句子,並將『動詞＋受格』或『介
　　 係詞＋受格』的部分劃上底線。

I.

1. <u>He likes</u> his dogs a lot.

2. But his neighbor doesn't like them, because <u>they bark</u> at him every day.

3. <u>I like</u> this movie, because <u>I think</u> it is interesting.

II.

1. The movie is about a farmer and <u>his neighbor</u>.

2. He likes <u>his dogs</u> a lot.

3. But <u>his neighbor</u> doesn't like them, because they bark at him every day.

III.

1. But his neighbor doesn't <u>like</u> <u>them</u>, because they bark <u>at</u> <u>him</u> every day.

My Best Friend

Tracy is my best friend. It is a cute dog. It does many things for me. It protects my home. It is loyal to my family. We love it a lot. However, it sometimes barks at our neighbors, so they feel angry at it. Maybe I should train it to stop barking.

我最好的朋友

崔西是我最好的朋友。牠是一隻可愛的狗。牠替我做了很多事。牠保護我家。牠對我的家人很忠心。我們很愛牠。然而,牠有時候會對我們的鄰居吠叫,因此他們對牠感到生氣。也許我應該訓練牠停止吠叫。

1. best 【bɛst】 形容詞 (good的最高級) 最好的

2. cute 【kjut】 形容詞 可愛的

3. does 【dʌz】 動詞 做 (原形為do，第三人稱單數及單數主詞使用)

4. for 【fɔr】 介係詞 替，為

5. protect 【prə`tɛkt】 動詞 保護

6. loyal 【`lɔɪəl】 形容詞 忠心的

7. love 【lʌv】 動詞 愛，疼愛

8. however 【haʊ`ɛvɚ】 副詞 然而

9. sometimes 【`sʌm,taɪmz】 副詞 有時候

10. so 【so】 對等連接詞 因此

11. feel 【fil】 動詞 感覺，覺得

12. angry 【`æŋgrɪ】 形容詞 生氣的

13. maybe 【`mebɪ】 副詞 也許

14. should 【ʃʊd】 助動詞 應該

15. train 【tren】 + 對象 + to 【tu】 + 原形V

    訓練…對象去做…

16. stop 【stɑp】 + V-ing　表停止某個正在進行中的動作

I. 請找出《實際運用短文 - My Best Friend》一文中有運用到「主格當主詞用：『主格＋be動詞』或『主格＋一般動詞』」的句子，並將『主格＋be動詞』或『主格＋一般動詞』的部分劃上底線。

II. 請找出《實際運用短文 - My Best Friend》一文中有運用到「所有格＋名詞」的句子，並將「所有格＋名詞」的部分劃上底線。

III. 請找出《實際運用短文 - My Best Friend》一文中有運用到「受格當受詞用：『動詞＋受格』或『介係詞＋受格』」的句子，並將『動詞＋受格』或『介係詞＋受格』的部分劃上底線。

I.

1. <u>It is</u> a cute dog.

2. <u>It does</u> many things for me.

3. <u>It protects</u> my home.

4. <u>It is</u> loyal to my family.

5. <u>We love</u> it a lot.

6. However, <u>it</u> sometimes <u>barks</u> at our neighbors, so <u>they feel</u> angry at it.

7. Maybe <u>I</u> should <u>train</u> it to stop barking.

II.

1. Tracy is <u>my</u> best <u>friend</u>.

2. It protects <u>my home</u>.

3. It is loyal to <u>my family</u>.

4. However, it sometimes barks at <u>our neighbors</u>, so they feel angry at it.

III.

1. It does many things <u>for me</u>.

2. We <u>love it</u> a lot.

3. However, it sometimes barks at our neighbors, so they feel angry <u>at it</u>.

4. Maybe I should <u>train it</u> to stop barking.

英文 ENGLISH
GRAMMAR 文法

不小心就 學會了

表「有」的用法

have和has的用法

主詞通常為可主動行使動作的生命物

*以下四種情況使用have：

(1)

| 第一人稱單、複數主詞 | I (我)／we (我們) + **have** |

例句1：I have a dream.

我有一個夢想。

例句2：We have two cars.

我們有兩輛車。

(2)

| 第二人稱單、複數主詞 | you (你，你們) + **have** |

例句1：You have many friends.

你有很多朋友。

例句2：You have much homework today.

你們今天有很多功課。

(3)

| 第三人稱複數主詞 | they (他們，她們，它們) + **have** |

例句：They have much money.

他們有很多錢。

(4)

| 複數主詞 | 例如：
John and Mary (約翰和瑪麗) + **have**
Mr. and Mrs. Wang (王先生和王太太) + **have** |

例句1：John and Mary have five guitars.

約翰和瑪麗有五把吉他。

例句2：Mr. and Mrs. Wang have two sons.

王先生和王太太有兩個兒子。

＊以下兩種情況使用has：

(1)

| 第三人稱單數 | he (他)／she (她)／it (它，牠) + **has** |

例句1：He has a motorcycle.

他有一輛摩托車。

例句2：She has beautiful eyes.

她有漂亮的雙眼。

例句3：It has some health problems.

牠有些健康問題。

(2)

| 單數人名 | 例如：David (大衛) + **has**
Helen (海倫) + **has**
Vicky (維琪) + **has** |

例句1：David has a computer.

大衛有一台電腦。

例句2：Vicky has a house.

維琪有一棟房屋。

實際運用短文 Track 006

Mr. and Mrs. Lin

Mr. and Mrs. Lin have a daughter and a son. Their daughter is five years old, and their son is eight years old. They have a house. Their house is very big. They have a pet dog. It has white hair. Mark and Kelly are their good friends. Mark has big eyes. Kelly has beautiful long hair.

林先生跟林太太

林先生跟林太太有一個女兒跟一個兒子。他們的女兒五歲，兒子八歲。他們有一棟房子。他們的房子很大。他們有一隻寵物狗。牠有白色的毛髮。馬克跟凱莉是他們的好朋友。馬克有雙大眼睛。凱莉有美麗的長頭髮。

1. Mr. 【`mɪstɚ】 名詞 先生

2. Mrs. 【`mɪsɪz】 名詞 夫人，太太

3. daughter 【`dɔtɚ】 名詞 女兒

4. son 【sʌn】 名詞 兒子

5. five 【faɪv】 名詞 五

6. year 【jɪr】 名詞 年，歲數

7. old 【old】 形容詞 老的，舊的

8. eight 【et】 名詞 八

9. house 【haʊs】 名詞 房子

10. big 【bɪg】 形容詞 大的

11. pet 【pɛt】 名詞 寵物

12. white 【hwaɪt】 形容詞 白色的

13. hair 【hɛr】 名詞 頭髮

14. eye 【aɪ】 名詞 眼睛

15. beautiful 【`bjutəfəl】 形容詞 美麗的

16. long 【lɔŋ】 形容詞 長的

17. hair 【hɛr】 名詞 頭髮

I. 請填入have或has

1. I _____ many dreams(夢想).

2. John's girlfriend _____ long hair.

3. Mr. and Mrs. Lin _____ a big house.

4. Linda _____ two pet dogs.

5. They _____ enough(足夠的) money.

II. 句子重組：請根據文法及句意，重組下列句子的部分，使成為完整正確的肯定直述句。

1. two daughters / have / Mr. and Mrs. Wang

2. Michael / a bicycle(腳踏車)/ has / a motorcycle(機車)/ and

3. many books / you / have

4. Helen / big / beautiful / eyes / has

5. some / health problems / has / she

III. 請找出《實際運用短文 - Mr. and Mrs. Lin》一文中有運用到「主詞 + have或主詞 + has」的句子，並將『主詞 + have』或『主詞 + has』的部分劃上底線。

解答

I.

1	have	2	has	3	have	4	has	5	have

II.

1. Mr. and Mrs. Wang have two daughters.

2. Michael has a bicycle and a motorcycle.

   或是Michael has a motorcycle and a bicycle.

3. You have many books.

4. Helen has beautiful big eyes.

5. She has some health problems.

III.

1. <u>Mr. and Mrs. Lin have</u> a daughter and a son.

2. <u>They have</u> a house.

3. <u>They have</u> a pet dog.

4. <u>It has</u> white hair.

5. <u>Mark has</u> big eyes.

6. <u>Kelly has</u> beautiful long hair.

重點二

there is／there are的用法

＊there + be動詞 (is / are) + 名詞 (片語) + 地方片語
此句型表「在…地方，有…人或物。」

＊be動詞要用is還是are要看其後的名詞 (片語) 而定

(1)

> there is + 單數名詞／不可數名詞 + 地方片語

例句：There is a book on the desk.

書桌上有一本書。

例句：There is some meat in the refrigerator.

冰箱裡有些肉。

(2)

> there are + 複數名詞 + 地方片語

例句1：There are many students in the classroom.

教室裡有很多學生。

例句2：There are two birds in the tree.

樹上有兩隻鳥。

(3)

> there + be動詞 (is/are) + Ving + 地方片語

表「某人(或動物)正在某地做…」

例句1：There is a boy singing in the classroom.

　　　有一個男孩在教室裡唱歌。

例句2：There are many people jogging in the park.

　　　有許多人在公園裡慢跑。

實際運用短文 ——————→ Track 007

Animals in the Zoo

　　Joe likes to go to the zoo with his friends because he likes animals. There are many animals in the zoo near his house. There are also many beautiful plants there. However, there are often many people there, and it becomes too noisy.

動物園裡的動物

　　喬喜歡跟他的朋友一起去動物園，因為他喜歡動物。他家附近的動物園有很多動物。那裡也有很多美麗的植物。然而，那裡常常充滿人潮，而變得太過吵雜。

1. go to + 地方　表「去…地方」

2. zoo 【zu】 名詞 動物園

3. because 【bɪ`kɔz】 連接詞 因為

4. animal 【`ænəm!】 名詞 動物

5. near 【nɪr】 介係詞 靠近

6. house 【haʊs】 名詞 家

7. also 【`ɔlso】 副詞 也

8. beautiful 【`bjutəfəl】 形容詞 美麗的

9. plant 【plænt】 名詞 植物

10. there 【ðɛr】 副詞 在那裡

11. however 【haʊ`ɛvə】 副詞 然而

12. often 【`ɔfən】 副詞 常常

13. people 【`pip!】 名詞 人們

14. become 【bɪ`kʌm】 動詞 變成

15. too 【tu】 副詞 太

16. noisy 【`nɔɪzɪ】 形容詞 喧鬧的，吵雜的

I. 請填入 there is 或 there are

1. _____ many dogs in the park.

2. _____ some water in the glass.

3. _____ two pictures on the wall.

4. _____ a bed in the room.

5. _____ some money in my pocket.

II. 句子重組：請根據文法及句意，重組下列句子的部分，
使成為完整正確的肯定直述句。

1. tea / there is / in the cup (杯子)

2. a man / sitting (坐著) / on the chair (椅子) / there is

3. playing balls (球) / many kids (小孩) / in the park / there are

4. many beautiful flowers (花朵) / there are / in the garden (花園)

5. there are / three teachers (老師) / in the office (辦公室) /
using (使用) the computers (電腦)

III. 請找出《實際運用短文 - Animals in the Zoo》一文中有
運用到「there + be動詞 (is / are) + 名詞 (片語) …」的句
子，並將『there + be動詞 (is / are) + 名詞 (片語)』的部
分劃上底線。

I.

1	There are
2	There is
3	There are
4	There is
5	There is

II.

1. There is tea in the cup.

2. There is a man sitting on the chair.

3. There are many kids playing balls in the park.

4. There are many beautiful flowers in the garden.

5. There are three teachers using the computers in the office.

III.

1. There are many animals in the zoo near his house.

2. There are also many beautiful plants there.

3. However, there are often many people there, and it becomes too noisy.

表「沒有」的句型

(1)

> 主詞 (I / you / we / they / 複數主詞) + don't【dont】
> + have

例句1： I don't have a car.

　　　我沒有車。

例句2： They don't have enough money.

　　　他們沒有足夠的錢。

例句3： Mr. and Mrs. Ho don't have any pet dogs.

　　　何先生和何太太沒有養任何寵物狗。

(2)

> 主詞 (he / she / it / 單數主詞) + doesn't【ˋdʌznt】
> + have

例句1： He doesn't have a pen.

　　　他沒有筆。

例句2： She doesn't have many English books.

　　　她沒有很多英文書。

例句3： It (= The book) doesn't have a cover (封面).

　　　它 (這本書) 沒有封面。

(3)

> there is + not + a 單數名詞 + 地方片語

例句1：There is not a mouse (老鼠) in the kitchen (廚房).
　　　廚房裡沒有老鼠。

例句2：There is not a school on the street.
　　　這條街上沒有學校。

(4)

> there is + not + 數量形容詞 + 不可數名詞 + 地方片語

例句1：There is not much milk in the bottle.
　　　瓶子裡沒有很多牛奶。

例句2：There is not any money in my pocket.
　　　我口袋裡沒有任何錢。

(5)

> there is + no + 不可數名詞 + 地方片語

例句1：There is no water (水) in the glass (玻璃杯).
　　　杯子裡沒有水。

例句2：There is no coffee (咖啡) in the cup (杯子).
　　　杯子裡沒有咖啡。

(6)

there are + no + 複數名詞 + 地方片語

例句1：There are no children here.

這裡沒有小孩。

例句2：There are no cars on the street.

這條街上沒有車子。

(7)

there are + not + 數量形容詞 + 複數名詞 + 地方片語

例句1：There are not many students in the classroom.

教室裡沒有很多學生。

例句2：There are not any books on the desk.

桌上沒有任何書。

Having a Dream

I don't have a dream now. My best friend Julia has a dream. She hopes to become a writer because she likes to read and write. I don't have any interest, so I don't know what I should do in the future. Mary is my classmate. She likes to chat with me. She doesn't have a dream, either. Maybe we will have our own dream someday when we find our interests.

擁有夢想

我現在沒有夢想。我最好的朋友茱麗葉擁有一個夢想。她希望成為作家，因為她喜歡閱讀和寫作。我沒有任何興趣，因此不知道未來應該做什麼。瑪莉是我的同學。她喜歡跟我聊天。她也沒有夢想。也許有一天當我們找到自己的興趣時，我們將會擁有自己的夢想。

1. dream【drim】 名詞 夢想

2. now【naʊ】 名詞 現在

3. best【bɛst】 形容詞最高級 最好的

4. hope【hop】+ to V 希望去…

5. become【bɪ`kʌm】 動詞 變成，成為

6. writer【`raɪtɚ】 名詞 作家

7. read【rid】 動詞 閱讀

8. write【raɪt】 動詞 寫

9. any【`ɛnɪ】 形容詞 任何的

10. interest【`ɪntərɪst】 名詞 興趣

11. 句子, so 句子. so 表因此，為對等連接詞，可連接兩個句子

12. know【no】 動詞 知道

13. what【hwɑt】 疑問代名詞 什麼

14. should【ʃʊd】 助動詞 應該

15. do【du】 動詞 做，行動

16. in the future【ɪn】【ðə】【`fjutʃɚ】 介係詞片語 在未來

17. classmate【`klæs,met】 名詞 同學

18. chat【tʃæt】 動詞 聊天

19. either【`iðɚ】 副詞 也

20. maybe【`mebɪ】 副詞 也許

21. someday【`sʌm,de】 副詞 未來有一天

22. 句子(,) when 句子.

　　when【hwɛn】為副詞連接詞，表「當…時」

23. find【faɪnd】**動詞** 找到，發現

練習題 ....

I. 請填入 don't 或 doesn't

1. I _____ have any ideas.

2. Johnson _____ have a car.

3. They _____ have any plans.

4. Mr. and Mrs. Wang _____ have any children.

5. It _____ have any effect(效果).

II. 請找出《實際運用短文 - Having a Dream》一文中有
　　運用到「don't + have 或 doesn't + have」的句子，並
　　將『don't + have 或 doesn't + have』的部分劃上底線。

解答

I.

1	don't
2	doesn't
3	don't
4	don't
5	doesn't

II.

1. I <u>don't have</u> a dream now.

2. I <u>don't have</u> any interest, so I <u>don't know</u> what I should do in the future.

3. She <u>doesn't have</u> a dream, either.

Track 009

There Are No Foods in the Refrigerator

Kelly is hungry. She wants to find something to eat, so she opens the refrigerator. However, there are not any foods in the refrigerator. There is no milk. There are no fruits. There is not a dish. Unluckily, there isn't any money in her pocket. She can't even buy snacks in a nearby convenient store. It's not her day!

冰箱裡沒有食物

凱莉肚子餓。她想要找些東西吃,所以她打開冰箱。然而,冰箱裡沒有任何食物。沒有牛奶。沒有水果。沒有菜餚。不幸的是,她口袋裡也沒有錢,連在附近的便利商店買點心都沒辦法。真是倒楣的一天!

1. food 【fud】 名詞 食物

2. refrigerator 【rɪ`frɪdʒə,retə】 名詞 冰箱

3. hungry 【`hʌŋgrɪ】 形容詞 飢餓的

4. want + to V 想要

5. find 【faɪnd】 動詞 發現，找到

6. eat 【it】 動詞 吃

7. open 【`opən】 動詞 打開

8. milk 【mɪlk】 名詞 牛奶

9. fruit 【frut】 名詞 水果

10. dish 【dɪʃ】 名詞 菜餚

11. unluckily 【ʌn`lʌkɪlɪ】 副詞 不幸地

12. money 【`mʌnɪ】 名詞 錢

13. pocket 【`pɑkɪt】 名詞 口袋

14. can't 【kænt】 = can not 助動詞 不能…

15. even 【`ivən】 副詞 甚至

16. buy 【baɪ】 動詞 買

17. snack 【snæk】 名詞 小吃，點心

18. nearby 【`nɪr,baɪ】 形容詞 附近的

19. convenient store 【kən`vinjənt】【stor】
名詞片語 便利商店

20. not + one's + day …人倒楣的日子

I. 中翻英

1. 桌上沒有任何書。

2. 辦公室裡沒有人。

3. 杯子裡沒有咖啡。

4. 公園裡連一隻貓也沒有。

5. 信箱裡一封信也沒有。

II. 請找出《實際運用短文 – There Are No Foods in the Refrigerator》一文中有運用到「there is + not + a 單數名詞；there is + not + 數量形容詞 + 不可屬名詞；there is + no + 不可屬名詞；there are + no + 複數名詞；或 there are + not + 數量形容詞 + 複數名詞」的句子，並將該部分劃上底線。

解答

I.

1	There are not any books on the desk.
2	There are no people in the office.
3	There is no coffee in the cup.
4	There is not even a cat in the park.
5	There is not a letter in the mailbox.

II.

1. However, <u>there are not any foods</u> in the refrigerator.

2. <u>There is no milk</u>.

3. <u>There are no fruits</u>.

4. <u>There is not a dish</u>.

5. Unluckily, <u>there</u> isn't <u>any money</u> in her pocket.

重點四

表「有」的疑問句型

(1)

> Do + I / you / we / they / 複數主詞 + have...?

例句1：Do you have a pen?

你有筆嗎？

例句2：Do they have credit cards?

他們有信用卡嗎？

(2)

> Does + he / she / it / 單數主詞 + have...?

例句1：Does she have a boyfriend?

她有男朋友嗎？

例句2：Does David have a car?

大衛有車嗎？

(3)

> Is + there + a 單數名詞 + 地方片語…?

例句1：Is there a teacher in the classroom?

教室裡有老師嗎？

例句2：Is there an error(錯誤) in the book?

書裡面有錯誤嗎？

*註：a＋子音為首的單字；an＋母音為首的單字

(4)

Is + there + (數量形容詞) + 不可數名詞 + 地方片語…?

例句1：Is there any water in the bottle?

瓶子裡有任何水嗎？

例句2：Is there much milk in the glass?

玻璃杯裡有很多牛奶嗎？

(5)

Are + there + (數量形容詞) + 複數名詞 + 地方片語…?

例句1：Are there many dogs in the park?

公園裡有很多狗嗎？

例句2：Are there any letters in the mailbox?

信箱裡有任何信嗎？

Do You Have Any Questions?

I am a teacher. I like to ask my students, "Do you have any questions?" Each time I ask them this, they often look shy or just say no. But I am not sure if they really mean it. Sometimes, they do have some questions, and are just too shy to raise any.

你有任何問題嗎？

我是一個老師。我喜歡問我的學生——「你們有任何問題嗎？」每一次我這樣問他們，他們常常是看起來害羞，或只是回答沒有。但我不確定他們是否真的沒有問題。有時候，他們的確有一些問題，只是過於害羞而未能提出。

重點註解 →

Track 010

1. question 【ˋkwɛstʃən】 名詞 問題
2. Each time 【itʃ】【taɪm】 + 句子, 句子.

   each time意思為「每次，每當」，為副詞連接詞，後可接兩個句子。

3. ask 【æsk】 動詞 問
4. this 【ðɪs】 代名詞 這(個)
5. often 【ˋɔfən】 副詞 通常，常常
6. look 【lʊk】 + 形容詞　看起來…

7. shy 【ʃaɪ】 形容詞 害羞的

8. or 【ɔr】 對等連接詞 或

9. just 【dʒʌst】 副詞 只是

10. say 【se】 動詞 說

11. but 【bʌt】 對等連接詞 但是

12. sure 【ʃʊr】 形容詞 確信的

13. if 【ɪf】 連接詞 是否

14. really 【ˋrɪəlɪ】 副詞 真地，確實

15. mean 【min】 動詞 意指

16. sometimes 【ˋsʌm,taɪmz】 副詞 有時候

17. do 【du】 / does 【dʌz】 / did 【dɪd】 + 原形動詞
    強調用法，表「的確⋯」

18. some 【sʌm】 形容詞 一些

19. just 【dʒʌst】 副詞 僅僅，只是

20. too + 形容詞／副詞 + to + 原形動詞　太⋯以致於不能⋯

21. raisc 【rez】 動詞 提出

練習題 ....

I. 中翻英

1. 麗莎有任何問題嗎？

2. 我們有足夠的錢嗎？

3. 王先生有車嗎？

4. 他有女朋友嗎？

5. 何先生和何太太有任何子女嗎？

II. 請找出《實際運用短文 - Do You Have Any Questions?》
一文中有運用到「Do + I / you / we / they / 複數主詞 +
have...?」或「Does + he / she / it / 單數主詞 + have...?」
的句子，並將該部分劃上底線。

解答

I.

1	Does Lisa have any questions?
2	Do we have enough money?
3	Does Mr. Wang have a car?
4	Does he have a girlfriend?
5	Do Mr. and Mrs. Ho have any children?

II.

1. I like to ask my students, "<u>Do you have</u> any questions?"

PART 04

How many,
How much 的用法

重點一：How many的用法

how many用來形成問句，意思為「多少？」需注意的是，
how many後面只能接「複數名詞」。

(1)

問句	How many + 複數名詞 + are there + 地方片語?
	在…地方有多少…東西？
答句1	There + is + (only只有) + a / one + 單數名詞 + 地方片語.
	在…地方有一個…東西。
答句2	There + are + 數量 + 複數名詞 + 地方片語.
	在…地方有多少個…東西。

例句1：

問 How many seasons(季節) are there in a year(年)？

一年有多少季節呢？

答 There are four seasons in a year.

一年有四季。

例句2：

問 How many students(學生) are there in the

classroom(教室)?

教室裡有多少學生呢？

答 There is only a student in the classroom.

教室裡只有一個學生。

(2)

問句	How many + 複數名詞 + do + I / you / we / they / 複數主詞 + have...?
	某人有多少…東西？
答句	I / You / We / They / 複數主詞 + have + 數量 + 名詞.
	某人有多少…東西。

例句1：

問 How many cats do you have?

你養幾隻貓？

答 I have two cats.

我養兩隻貓。

例句2：

問 How many apples do they have?

他們有幾顆蘋果？

答 They have ten apples.

他們有十顆蘋果。

(3)

問句	How many + 複數名詞 + does + he / she / it / 單數主詞 + have...?
	某人有多少…東西？
答句	He / She / It / 單數主詞 + has + 數量 + 名詞.
	某人有多少…東西。

例句1：

問 How many pens does Mary have?

瑪莉有幾隻筆？

答 She has five pens.

她有五隻筆。

例句2：

問 How many children does Mr. Chen have?

陳先生有幾個小孩？

答 He has three children.

他有三個小孩。

重點二：How much的用法

how much用來形成問句，意思為「多少？」需注意的是，how much後面只能接「不可數名詞」。

(1)

問句	How much + 不可數名詞 + is there + 地方片語?
	在…地方有多少…東西？
答句	There + is + no(沒有) / little(很少，幾乎沒有) / a little (一些) / much(很多) / a lot of (很多) + 不可數名詞 + 地方片語.
	在…地方有多少…東西。

例句1：

問 How much garbage(垃圾) is there in the living room(客廳)?

客廳裡有多少垃圾?

答 There is little garbage in the living room.

客廳裡幾乎沒有垃圾。

例句2：

問 How much money is there in your pocket(口袋)?

你口袋裡有多少錢?

答 There is no money in my pocket.

我口袋裡沒有錢。

(2)

問句	How much + 不可數名詞 + do + I / you / we / they / 複數主詞 + 原形動詞…? 某人…多少…東西?
答句	I / You / We / They / 複數主詞 + 原形動詞 + no(沒有) / little(很少，幾乎沒有) / a little(一些) / much(很多) / a lot of (很多) + 不可數名詞. 某人…多少…東西。

例句1：

問 How much sugar do you need for your black tea?

你的紅茶需要多少糖?

答 I need much sugar for my black tea.

我的紅茶需要很多糖。

例句2：

問 How much money do they need for the plan?

這個計劃他們需要多少錢？

答 They need a lot of money for the plan.

他們這個計劃需要很多錢。

(3)

問句	How much + 不可數名詞 + does + he / she / it / 單數主詞 + 原形動詞…?
	某人…多少…東西？
答句	He / She / It / 單數主詞 + 原形動詞 (字尾加 s / es 或去 y 加 ies) + no (沒有) / little (很少，幾乎沒有) / a little (一些) / much (很多) / a lot of (很多) + 不可數名詞.
	某人…多少…東西。

例句1：

問 How much butter does Linda need for the dish?

琳達這道菜需要多少奶油？

答 She needs little butter for the dish.

她這道菜幾乎不需要奶油。

例句2：

問 How much pork does he need for the dish?

他這道菜需要多少豬肉？

答 He needs a lot of pork for the dish.

他這道菜需要很多豬肉。

A Good Waiter

A good waiter needs to know the answers to the following questions: "How many guests are there in the restaurant?", "How many seats are there in the restaurant?", "How much water should I pour in a glass?", "How many dishes does a guest usually order?", and "How much time does the cook need for each dish?"

It is lucky to meet a good waiter because service is sure to be great. When you do, never forget to tip well.

好服務生

一個好服務生需要知道下列問題的答案:「餐廳裡有多少客人?」「餐廳裡有多少位子?」「杯裡應該倒入多少水?」「一個客人通常點多少菜?」「廚師料理每道菜需要多少時間?」

遇見好服務生是幸運的,因為服務肯定很棒。當你遇見時,別忘了要好好給小費。

1. waiter【`wetɚ】 名詞 服務生

2. need【nid】+ to V 需要去做…

3. know【no】 動詞 知道

4. answer【`ænsɚ】 名詞 答案

5. following【`faləwɪŋ】 形容詞 下列的

6. question【`kwɛstʃən】 名詞 問題

7. guest【gɛst】 名詞 客人

8. restaurant【`rɛstərənt】 名詞 餐廳

9. seat【sit】 名詞 座位

10. water【`wɔtɚ】 名詞 水

11. pour【por】 動詞 倒

12. glass【glæs】 名詞 玻璃杯

13. dish【dɪʃ】 名詞 菜餚

14. usually【`juʒʊəlɪ】 副詞 通常

15. order【`ɔrdɚ】 動詞 點菜

16. time【taɪm】 名詞 時間

17. cook【kʊk】 名詞 廚師

18. each【itʃ】 形容詞 每一，各自的

19. lucky【`lʌkɪ】 形容詞 幸運的

20. meet【mit】 動詞 遇見

21. 句子(,) + because + 句子. because意思為「因為」，為副詞連接詞，可放句中連接兩個句子。

22. service 【ˋsɝvɪs】 名詞 服務

23. sure 【ʃʊr】 形容詞 必定的

   be sure to + V 表「一定…」

24. great 【gret】 形容詞 美妙的，極好的

25. When 【hwɛn】 + 句子, 句子. when意思為「當…」，為

   副詞連接詞，可放句首，後面接兩個句子。

26. do/does/did 可代替前面提過的動詞片語。

   do在此代替前面的動詞片語meet a good waiter

27. never 【ˋnɛvɚ】 副詞 決不

28. forget 【fɚˋgɛt】 + to V 忘記去做…事

29. tip 【tɪp】 動詞 給小費

30. well 【wɛl】 副詞 很好地，滿意地

I. 中翻英

1. 你錢包裡有多少錢?

2. 抽屜裡有多少封信?

3. 一年有多少天?

4. 你需要多少零用錢?

5. 動物園裡有多少隻老虎?

II. 請找出《實際運用短文 - A Good Waiter》一文中有運用到「How many + 名詞…? 或How much + 名詞…?」的句子,並將該部分劃上底線。

III. 選擇題

1. How many pictures(圖片) _____ there on the wall?

   (A) is　(B) are　(C) have (D) do

2. How much butter(奶油) _____ Mary need?

   (A) is　(B) are　(C) does (D) do

3. How much pork(豬肉) _____ there in the refrigerator?

   (A) is　(B) are　(C) does (D) do

4. How _____ foreigners(外國人) are there in the classroom?

   (A) many (B) much (C) old (D) often

5. How _____ sugar does he need for the green tea(綠茶)?

   (A) many (B) much (C) old (D) long

I.

1	How much money is there in your purse(錢包)?
2	How many letters are there in the drawer?
3	How many days are there in a year?
4	How much pocket money do you need?
5	How many tigers(老虎) are there in the zoo?

II.

1. A good waiter needs to know the answers to the following questions: "How many guests are there in the restaurant?", "How many seats are there in the restaurant?", "How much water should I pour in a glass?", "How many dishes does a guest usually order?", and "How much time does the cook need for each dish?"

III.

| 1 | B | 2 | C | 3 | A | 4 | A | 5 | B |

英文 ENGLISH
GRAMMAR 文法
不小心就 學會了

How old,
How tall 的用法

重點一：How old的用法

old【old】形容詞 老的，…歲的。

「How old...?」用來詢問年齡，意思為「…年紀多大?」

(1)

問句	How old + is + he / she / it / 單數主詞?
答句	He / She / It / 單數主詞 + is + 數字 + (years old).

例句1：

問 How old is your father? 您父親年紀多大?

答 He is fifty years old. 他五十歲。

例句2：

問 How old is she? 她年紀多大?

答 She is thirty years old. 她三十歲。

(2)

問句	How old + are + you / we / they / 複數主詞?	
答句	You / We / They / 複數主詞 + are 或 I + am	+ 數字 + (years old).

例句1：

問 How old are you? 你年紀多大?

答 I am twenty years old. 我二十歲。

例句2：

問 How old are your students? 你的學生們年紀多大？

答 They are between 15 to 18 years old. 他們介於十五到十八歲。

重點二：How tall 的用法

tall【tɔl】 形容詞 高的，身高…的。

「How tall...?」用來詢問身高，意思為「…有多高?」

(1)

問句	How tall + is + he / she / it / 單數主詞?
答句	He / She / It / 單數主詞 + is + 數字 + feet(英尺) / centimeters(公分) + tall.

例句1：

問 How tall is the tree? 這棵樹有多高？

答 It is five feet tall. 它五英尺高。

例句2：

問 How tall is he? 他多高？

答 He is 175 centimeters tall. 他身高175公分。

(2)

問句	How tall + are + you / we / they / 複數主詞?	
答句	You / We / They / 複數主詞 + are 或 I + am	+ 數字 + feet(英尺) / centimeters(公分) + tall.

英文文法 不輸 **學會了**

例句1：

問 How tall are you? 你有多高?

答 I am 168 centimeters tall. 我身高168公分。

例句2：

問 How tall are they? 他們多高?

答 They are 180 centimeters tall. 他們身高180公分。

實際運用短文 → Track 012

My Best Friend

My best friend is Luna. She is my classmate. She is 20 years old. And she is 160 centimeters tall. She likes to talk with me. We often study English together because we both like English. Luna doesn't like to play basketball, for she thinks she is too short. But I like to play basketball a lot. I am 175 centimeters tall, so I am tall enough to play basketball well.

我最好的朋友

我最好的朋友是露娜。她是我的同學。她二十歲。而她身高一百六十公分。她喜歡跟我說話。我們常常一起讀英文，因為我們都喜歡英文。露娜不喜歡打籃球，因為她覺得自己太矮。但是我很喜歡打籃球。我身高一百七十五公分，因此有足夠的高度打好籃球。

重點註解 Track 012

1. year【jɪr】 名詞 年紀，歲數

2. old【old】 形容詞 …歲的，老的

3. centimeter【`sɛntə,mitɚ】 名詞 公分

4. tall【tɔl】 形容詞 …高的

5. talk with + 人　跟某人說話

6. often【`ɔfən】 副詞 常常

7. study【`stʌdɪ】 (動詞) 學習

8. 句子, because 句子.　because為副詞連接詞，前後可接兩個句子。

9. both【boθ】 副詞 兩者皆

10. however【haʊ`ɛvɚ】 副詞 然而

11. doesn't【`dʌzn̩t】 (= does not) + V　現在簡單式的否定句

12. play + 運動名稱　打…球，play basketball為打籃球的意思

13. 句子, for 句子.　for為對等連接詞，可連接兩個句子，表「因為」

14. think【θɪŋk】 動詞 想，認為

15. too【tu】 副詞 太…

16. short【ʃɔrt】 形容詞 矮的

17. but【bʌt】 對等連接詞 但是

18. a lot (這裡可以等於very much)　副詞片語 很多

19. 形容詞／副詞 + enough【ə`nʌf】 + to + V　足夠…去…

20. well【wɛl】 副詞 好地

I. 中翻英

1. 令尊年紀多大?

2. 他六十歲。

3. 你弟弟多高?

4. 他身高一八〇。

5. 你的狗幾歲了?

II. 請找出《實際運用短文 - My Best Friend》一文中有運用到「主詞 + be ...old.或主詞 + be...tall.」的句子，並將該部分劃上底線。

III. 選擇題

1. A: How _____ is your uncle(叔叔)?

   B: He is forty(四十) years old.

   (A) old   (B) tall   (C) young   (D) many

2. A: How _____ is your daughter(女兒)?

   B: She is 165 centimeters tall.

   (A) old   (B) tall   (C) young   (D) many

3. A: How old is your grandmother(祖母)?

   B: She is ninety(九十) _____.

   (A) feet tall   (B) old   (C) years old   (D) many years

4. A: How tall is the table (桌子)?

B: It is 100 _____ tall.

(A) words   (B) letters   (C) years   (D) centimeters

5. A: How old is your cat?

B: _____ 3 years old.

(A) It is   (B) They are   (C) I am   (D) You are

解答

I.

1	How old is your father?
2	He is sixty years old.
3	How tall is your younger brother?
4	He is 180 centimeters tall.
5	How old is your dog?

II.

1. She is 20 years old.

2. And she is 160 centimeters tall.

3. I am 175 centimeters tall, so I am tall enough to play basketball well.

III.

| 1 | A | 2 | B | 3 | C | 4 | D | 5 | A |

英文文法秒學會了   91

英文 ENGLISH
GRAMMAR 文法
不小心就 學會了

現在簡單式

重點一：使用時機

一、表示現在的動作或狀態

例句1：Mary sings very well.

瑪莉唱歌很好聽。

例句2：John likes to play basketball.

約翰喜歡打籃球。

例句3：It rains a lot in Taipei.

台北多雨。

二、不變的事實或真理

例句1：The sun rises in the east.

太陽從東邊上升。

例句2：The earth goes around the sun.

地球繞著太陽跑。

例句3：Water freezes at zero degrees Centigrade【`sɛntə͵gred】.

水攝氏零度時結冰。

三、表示一種習慣(常與頻率副詞或時間副詞連用)

＊頻率副詞：always(總是), usually(經常), often(常常),
sometimes(有時候), seldom(很少), never(從不)

＊時間副詞：every + morning / summer / Sunday / day
(每個早上/每個夏天/每個星期天/每天)

例句1：I <u>often</u> go to the movies every Sunday (= on Sundays).

我常在周日去看電影。

例句2：My father goes jogging <u>every morning</u>.

我爸爸每天早上慢跑。

例句3：I <u>usually</u> go to work by bus.

我經常搭公車上班。

例句4：She <u>always</u> plays the guitar when she is free.

她有空時就彈吉他。

例句5：He <u>never</u> takes a rest after lunch.

他午餐後從不休息。

例句6：David takes a trip <u>every summer</u>.

大衛夏天都會去旅行。

例句7：Mark <u>seldom</u> plays baseball with his son.

馬克很少跟他的兒子打棒球。

重點二：現在簡單式裡動詞的變化

1. 主詞 (you / we / they / 複數主詞) + 原形動詞

例句1：They take exercise every evening.

他們傍晚都會去運動。

例句2：My classmates play baseball every day.

我的同學每天打棒球。

例句3：We sometimes listen to the music when we are free.

我們有空的時候有時候會聽音樂。

2. 主詞 (he / she / it / 單數主詞) + 動詞 (字尾加上s或es或去y加上ies)

＊注意：不規則變化「have→has」

例句1：Vicky drinks tea every day.

維琪每天喝茶。

【原形動詞drink，字尾加上s】

例句2：He goes to work by MRT (捷運) every morning.

他每天早上搭捷運去上班。

【原形動詞go，字尾加上es】

例句3：She studies English every Saturday.

她每周六學習英文。

【原形動詞study，去掉字尾y加上ies】

3. 變化表：

一般動詞 （原形）	現在簡單式 （字尾加s）	中文意思	變化後動詞 的音標
close	closes	關上	【klosɪz】
move	moves	移動，搬家	【muvz】
like	likes	喜歡	【laɪks】

use	uses	使用	【jusɪz】
open	opens	打開	【`opənz】
play	plays	玩	【plez】
talk	talks	說話	【tɔks】
ask	asks	問	【æsks】
jump	jumps	跳	【dʒʌmps】
call	calls	打電話，稱呼	【kɔlz】
listen	listens	聽	【`lɪsənz】

一般動詞 (原形)	現在簡單式 (字尾加 es) 【註解：o、 x、s、z、ch、 sh 結尾的字】	中文意思	變化後動詞 的音標
do	does	做	【dʌz】
go	goes	去	【goz】
pass	passes	經過	【pæsɪz】
buzz	buzzes	嗡嗡叫	【bʌzɪz】
watch	watches	觀看	【wʊtʃɪz】
wash	washes	洗	【waʃɪz】

英文文法 不小就學會了

一般動詞 (原形)	現在簡單式 (去y加上 ies) 【註解:動詞字尾是「子音+y」時,須先去掉 y,再加 ies】	中文意思	變化後動詞 的音標
fly	flies	飛	【flaɪz】
study	studies	學習,研究	【`stʌdɪz】
try	tries	嘗試	【traɪz】

重點三:現在簡單式的疑問句型

1. Do + 主詞 (you/I/we/they/複數名詞) + 原形動詞…?

例句1:Do you play basketball after school every day?
　　　你每天放學後打籃球嗎?

例句2:Do they go jogging every morning?
　　　他們每天早上去慢跑嗎?

例句3:Do John and Mary go to work by MRT?
　　　約翰和瑪莉搭捷運上班嗎?

2. Does + 主詞 (he/she/it/單數名詞) + 原形動詞…?

例句1：Does Lisa play the piano?

麗莎彈鋼琴嗎?

例句2：Does he go to the concert every month?

他每個月去音樂會嗎?

例句3：Does it rain a lot in Taiwan?

台灣多雨嗎?

重點四：現在簡單式的否定句型

＊主詞(you/I/we/they/複數名詞) + do not/don't + 原形動詞…

例句1：I don't cook dinner every evening.

我沒有每個晚上煮飯。

例句2：They don't have a car.

他們沒有車。

＊主詞(he/she/it/單數名詞) + does not/doesn't + 原形動詞…

例句1：Helen doesn't like to sing songs in English.

海倫不喜歡用英文唱歌。

例句2：He doesn't drive to work.

他不開車上班。

Track 013

Music Lovers

My name is Kelly. I like music a lot. I often play the piano on weekends, and I practice the guitar every day. My roommate May likes music, too. She is an elementary school teacher, and she teaches music at a school. She always plays the piano when she has free time. However, she doesn't like to sing because she thinks her voice is not good. But she listens to pop songs and classical music every night after work. Sometimes we practice the piano together, but we don't sing songs together. All of our friends call us "music lovers," because we both love music so much.

音樂愛好者

我的名字是凱莉。我很喜歡音樂。我常常在週末彈鋼琴，而且我每天練習吉他。我的室友梅也喜歡音樂。她是一個國小老師，她在學校教音樂。她有空時總是彈鋼琴。然而，她不喜歡唱歌，因為她覺得自己的歌喉不好。但是她每天晚上下班後聽流行音樂跟古典音樂。有時候我們一起練習鋼琴，但是沒有一起唱歌。所有我們的朋友都說我們是「音樂愛好者」，因為我們兩個都這麼喜愛音樂。

1. music 【`mjuzɪk】 名詞 音樂

2. lover 【`lʌvɚ】 名詞 愛好者，熱愛者

3. name 【nem】 名詞 名字

4. often 【`ɔfən】 副詞 常常

5. play + the + 樂器名稱　彈奏…樂器

6. weekend 【`wik`ɛnd】 名詞 周末

　　on weekends = every weekend 每逢周末

7. practice 【`præktɪs】 動詞 練習

8. roommate 【`rum,met】 名詞 室友

9. elementary 【,ɛlə`mɛntərɪ】 形容詞 初級的，基礎的

10. school 【skul】 名詞 學校

11. teacher 【`titʃɚ】 名詞 老師

12. teach 【titʃ】 動詞 教書

13. always 【`ɔlwez】 副詞 總是

14. piano 【pɪ`æno】 名詞 鋼琴

15. free 【fri】 形容詞 自由的，空閒的

16. time 【taɪm】 名詞 時間

17. sing 【sɪŋ】 動詞 唱歌

18. think 【θɪŋk】 動詞 想，認為

19. voice 【vɔɪs】 名詞 聲音，嗓子

20. listen 【`lɪsn̩】 (+ to) 動詞 聽

21. pop 【pɑp】 形容詞 流行的

22. song【sɔŋ】 名詞 歌

23. classical【`klæsɪk!】 形容詞 古典的

24. night【naɪt】 名詞 晚上

25. after work 介係詞片語 下班後

26. sometimes【`sʌm,taɪmz】 副詞 有時候

27. together【tə`gɛðə】 副詞 一起

28. 句子, but 句子. but為對等連接詞，可前後連接兩個句子。

29. all【ɔl】 代名詞 全體，一切

30. call【kɔl】 動詞 稱呼，叫做

31. so【so】 副詞 如此，這麼

練習題

I. 中翻英

1. 你喜歡喝茶嗎?

2. 英格麗喜歡彈鋼琴。

3. 我爸媽每天早上去公園散步。

4. 他們每年出國一次嗎?

5. 她每周二晚上上吉他課。

II. 請找出《實際運用短文 - Music Lovers》一文中有運
　　用到「現在簡單式否定句型」的句子，並將該部分劃
　　上底線。

III. 選擇題

1. Water _____ at 100 degrees Centigrade.

   (A) boiled   (B) is boiled   (C) boils (D) boiling

2. I _____ to the concert every two months.

   (A) went   (B) going   (C) go   (D) am going

3. _____ your students like English?

   (A) Do   (B) Does   (C) Are (D) Is

4. Sally _____ the dishes after dinner.

   (A) don't wash (B) doesn't wash (C) wash (D) be washing

5. Mr. Ho _____ two cars now (現在).

   (A) have   (B) has   (C) had (D) is having

解答

I.

1	Do you like to drink tea?
2	Ingrid likes to play the piano.
3	My parents take a walk in the park every morning.
4	Do they go abroad once a year?
5	She goes to the guitar class every Tuesday (= on Tuesdays).

Part
6

II.

1. However, she <u>doesn't like</u> to sing because she thinks her voice is not good.

2. Sometimes we practice the piano together, but we <u>don't sing</u> songs together.

III.

1	C	2	C	3	A	4	B	5	B

How often,
How long 的用法

重點一：How often的用法

often 【`ɔfən】 副詞 常常。

「How often...?」用來詢問做一件事情的頻率，意思為「多常...?」此句型常與「次數，時間片語，或頻率副詞合用」。

1.

問句	How often + do + I / you / we / they / 複數主詞 + 原形動詞...?
答句	I / You / We / They / 複數主詞 + 原形動詞...(+次數) + 時間片語.

*次數：
once (一次) / twice (兩次)，三次以上用「數目字 + times：three times (三次) / four times (四次)...」

*時間片語：
every week / month / year (每周/每個月/每年)，a week / month / year (一周/一個月/一年)，every two weeks / months / years (每兩周/每兩個月/每兩年)

*頻率副詞：
always (總是)，usually (經常)，often (常常)，sometimes (有時候)，seldom (很少)，never (從不)

例句1：

問 How often do they go jogging?

他們多久慢跑一次？

答 They go jogging every month.

他們每個月都去慢跑。

例句2：

問 How often do you play basketball?

你多久打籃球一次？

答 I play basketball once a week.

我一個禮拜打一次。

例句3：

問 How often do Mary and John go to the park?

瑪莉跟約翰多久去公園一次？

答 They go to the park three times every month.

他們每個月去公園三次。

例句4：

問 How often do the students go abroad?

學生們多久出國一次？

答 They go abroad once a year.

他們一年出國一次。

2.

問句	How often + does + he / she / it / 單數主詞 + 原形動詞…?
答句	He / She / It / 單數主詞 + 動詞 (字尾加上s或es或去y加上ies)… (+次數) + 時間片語.

例句1：

問 How often does he go to the movies?

他多久看電影一次？

答 He goes to the movies twice a month.

他一個月看電影兩次。

例句2：

問 How often does your father walk the dog?

令尊多久遛狗一次？

答 He walks the dog every day.

他每天遛狗。

例句3：

問 How often does it rain in Kaohsiung(高雄) in winter?

高雄冬天多久下雨一次？

答 It seldom rains in Kaohsiung in winter.

高雄冬天很少下雨。

例句4：

問 How often does your student Kevin fall asleep（睡著）
in your class?

你的學生凱文多常在課堂上睡著？

答 He never falls asleep in my class.

他上我的課從未睡著。

重點二：How long的用法

long【lɔŋ】 形容詞 長的，長久的。

「How long...?」用來詢問做一件事情有多久，意思為
「…多久？」，此句型常與「for + 一段時間」合用。

1.

問句	How long + do + I / you / we / they / 複數主詞 + 原形動詞…?
答句	I / You / We / They / 複數主詞 + 原形動詞… + for + 一段時間…

Part 7

例句1：

問 How long do you study English every day?

你每天念英文多久？

答 I study English for two hours every day.

我每天念英文兩個小時。

例句2：

問 How long do your students practice the guitar every week?

你的學生每周練習吉他多久？

答 They practice the guitar for two days every week.

他們每周練習吉他兩天。

2.

問句	How long + does + he / she / it / 單數主詞 + 原形動詞…?
答句	He / She / It / 單數主詞 + 動詞(字尾加上 s 或 es 或去 y 加上 ies)… + for + 一段時間…

例句1：

問 How long does she listen to the music every day?

她每天聽音樂多久？

答 She listens to the music for 30 minutes(分鐘) every day.

她每天聽音樂三十分鐘。

例句2：

問 How long does the class last every Friday night?

這堂課每周五晚上持續多久？

答 It lasts for 3 hours every Friday night.

它每周五晚上持續三個小時。

Going to a Sports Park

Mark is a salesman. He goes to work by bus every day. He often has to work overtime, so he has no time to exercise on weekdays. Therefore, he usually goes to a sports park near his house on weekends. He goes there about three times a month, and he always exercises there for more than 2 hours.

Are you a busy office worker like Mark? How often do you go to a sports park? And how long do you exercise there? Maybe it's better for you to exercise at least three times in a sports park every week.

去運動公園

馬克是一個業務員。他每天搭公車上班。他常常必須加班,所以他平日沒有時間運動。因此他經常在週末時去家附近的運動公園。他一個月大約去三次,在那裡運動超過兩個小時。

你跟馬克一樣是一個忙碌的上班族嗎?你多久去運動公園一次?在那裡運動多久的時間?也許每周至少去運動公園運動三次對你是比較好的。

1. sports 【spɔrts】 形容詞 運動的

2. park 【pɑrk】 名詞 公園

3. salesman 【ˋselzmən】 名詞 推銷員，業務員

4. go to work 動詞片語 去上班

5. by + 交通工具 搭乘…交通工具

6. often 【ˋɔfən】 副詞 常常

7. have to + V 必須…

8. overtime 【ˋovɚ͵taɪm】 副詞 超過時間，加班地

9. exercise 【ˋɛksɚ͵saɪz】 動詞 運動

10. weekend 【ˋwikˋɛnd】 名詞 周末

11. about + 數目字 大約…

12. time 【taɪm】 名詞 次，回

13. month 【mʌnθ】 名詞 月

14. always 【ˋɔlwez】 副詞 總是

15. for + 一段時間 表「經歷…多久的時間」

16. more than 表「超過」= over

17. hour 【aʊr】 名詞 小時

18. busy 【ˋbɪzɪ】 形容詞 忙碌的

19. office worker 【ˋɔfɪs】【ˋwɝkɚ】 名詞片語 上班族

20. like 【laɪk】 介係詞 像

21. there 【ðɛr】 副詞 在那裡

22. maybe 【ˋmebɪ】 副詞 或許

23. better 【`bɛtɚ】 形容詞比較級 比較好 (good / better / best)

24. at least 【æt】【list】 介係詞片語 至少

25. week 【wik】 名詞 週，星期

練習題

I. 中翻英

1. 他們多久練習籃球一次?

2. 我們每周練習籃球三次。

3. 電影通常撥放多久?

4. 它通常撥放兩個小時。

5. 大衛每週至少在運動公園運動五次。

II. 請找出《實際運用短文 - Going to a Sports Park》一文中有運用到「主詞+原形動詞 (s/es/ies)…(+次數)+時間片語」的句子，並將該部分劃上底線。

III. 選擇題

1. A: How _____ do you play tennis(網球)?

   B: Three times a week.

   (A) long   (B) often   (C) well   (D) old

2. A: How _____ does the concert usually last?

   B: It usually lasts for two hours.

   (A) long   (B) often   (C) well   (D) old

3. Lisa sometimes _____ to school on foot(走路).

   (A) go   (B) went   (C) goes   (D) going

英文文法 秘 學會了

4. Vincent _____ English every day.

  (A) study (B) studies (C) studied (D) studying

5. How often _____ your parents go abroad(出國)?

  (A) do (B) does (C) doing (D) done

解答

I.

1	How often do they practice basketball?
2	We practice basketball three times a week.
3	How long does the movie usually last?
4	It usually lasts for two hours.
5	David exercises in the sports park at least five times every week.

II.

1. He goes to work by bus every day.

2. He often has to work overtime, so he has no time to exercise on weekdays.

3. Therefore, he usually goes to a sports park near his house on weekends.

4. He goes there about three times a month, and he always exercises there for more than 2 hours.

III.

1	B	2	A	3	C	4	B	5	A

搭乘交通工具
的用法

重點一

使用一般動詞(片語)來表達,常見的有:

drive(開車,駕駛),walk(走路),fly(搭飛機),sail(搭船),bike(騎單車),ride a bike(騎單車),ride a motorcycle(騎機車),take the bus(搭公車),take the train(搭火車),take the MRT(搭捷運),take the subway(搭地下鐵)

重點二

使用「by + 交通工具」來表達,常見的有:

by car(搭車,開車),by bus(搭公車),by train(搭火車),by subway / metro / tube(搭地鐵),by MRT(搭捷運),by plane / by air(搭飛機),by boat(搭船),by bicycle(騎單車)

※例外:on foot(走路)

重點三

詢問對方如何搭乘交通工具的句型為:

1.

問句	How + do + I/you/we/they/複數主詞 + go to 地方…?
答句1	I/You/We/They/複數主詞 + go to 地方 + by 交通工具 / on foot

答句2	I/You/We/They/複數主詞 + 一般動詞(+交通工具) + to 地方/to 原形動詞…

例句1：

問 How do you go to work? 你怎麼上班？

答1 I go to work by bus. 我搭公車上班。

答2 I take a bus to work. 我搭公車上班。

例句2：

問 How do your students go to school?

你的學生怎麼上學？

答1 They go to school by MRT.

他們搭捷運上學。

答2 They takes the MRT to school.

他們搭捷運上學。

2.

問句	How + does + he/she/it/單數主詞+ go to 地方…?
答句1	He/She/It/單數主詞+ goes to 地方 + by 交通工具/ on foot
答句2	He/She/It/單數主詞+ 一般動詞(字尾加上s/es，或去y加上ies) (+交通工具) + to 地方/ to 原形動詞…

例句1：

問 How does she go to the park? 她怎麼去公園？

答1 She goes to the park by car. 她開車去公園。

答2 She drives to the park. 她開車去公園。

英文文法 不知不覺 學會了　　　117

例句2：

問 How does your father go to the office?

令尊怎麼到辦公室？

答1 He goes to the office on foot.

他走路來辦公室。

答2 He walks to the office.

他走路來辦公室。

實際運用短文 Track 015

Riding Your Bicycle to Work

How do you go to work? Many people in Taipei go to work by bus or by MRT. However, if your office is not far from your house, maybe you can ride your bicycle to work. For one thing, it is good for health. For another, it saves money. And it is good for environmental protection, too. Why not give it a try next time!?

騎腳踏車上班

你怎麼上班呢？台北許多人搭公車或捷運上班。然而，如果辦公室離你家不遠，也許你可以騎腳踏車上班。一來對健康有益。二來可以省錢。而且也有助於環保。下次何不試試看呢！？

1. ride【raɪd】 動詞 騎，搭乘

2. bicycle【`baɪsɪk!】 名詞 腳踏車

3. work【wɜk】 動詞 工作

4. go to work 動詞片語 上班

5. bus【bʌs】 名詞 公車

6. MRT = Mass Rapid Transit　大眾捷運系統

　 mass【mæs】 形容詞 大眾的

　 rapid【`ræpɪd】 形容詞 迅速的

　 transit【`trænsɪt】 名詞 公共交通運輸系統

7. office【`ɔfɪs】 名詞 辦公室

8. far from【fɑr】【frɑm】 離…很遠

　 far【fɑr】 形容詞 遠的

9. maybe【`mebɪ】 副詞 也許

10. for one thing【θɪŋ】 ... ; for another【ə`nʌðə】
　 一來…，二來…

11. save【sev】 動詞 節省，儲蓄

12. environmental【ɪn,vaɪrən`mɛnt!】 形容詞 環境的

13. protection【prə`tɛkʃən】 名詞 保護

14. too【tu】 副詞 也

15. why not + 原形動詞…?　何不…?

16. give it a try （動詞片語）試一試

　　give【gɪv】（動詞）給，做⋯動作；

　　try【traɪ】（名詞）嘗試

17. next time【ˋnɛkst】【taɪm】（時間片語）下一次

練習題

I. 連貫式翻譯

1. 大衛在一家電腦公司上班。

2. 他每天通常開車上班。

3. 偶爾他會搭公車上班。

4. 下班後他常常在公園慢跑。

5. 公園離他家不遠，所以他都走路過去。

II. 請找出《實際運用短文 - Riding Your Bicycle to Work》
　 一文中有運用到「go to 地方 + by 交通工具，或一般
　 動詞（+ 交通工具）+ to 地方/to 原形動詞⋯」表搭乘
　 交通工具的句子，並將該部分劃上底線。

III. 選擇題

1. A: _____ does Bill go to school?

　 B: He walks to school.

　 (A) When　(B) How　　(C) What　　　(D) Why

2. How _____ your parents go to the park?

    (A) does   (B) do   (C) often   (D) are

3. Vincent, my student, _____ to my English class on foot.

    (A) goes   (B) go   (C) walk   (D) walks

4. A: How do you go there?

    B: I plan to _____ there.

    (A) foot   (B) train   (C) drive   (D) car

5. A: How do the students go to school?

    B: _____.

    (A) By bus   (B) At 6:30   (C) Near the park   (D) By the way

解答

I.

1	David works at a computer company.
2	He usually drives to work every day. / He usually goes to work by car every day.
3	Sometimes he takes a bus to work. / Sometimes he goes to work by bus.
4	He often goes jogging in a park after work.
5	The park is not far from his house, so he always walks there. / The park is not far from his house, so he always goes there on foot.

II.

1. Many people in Taipei <u>go to work by bus or by MRT</u>.

2. However, if your office is not far from your house, maybe you can <u>ride your bicycle to work</u>.

III.

1	B	2	B	3	A	4	C	5	A

時間、星期
和四季

重點一

What time...?用於詢問時間(time【taɪm】 名詞 時間)。

句型如下：

1.

問句	What time is it? 現在幾點？
答句1	It is + 數字 + o'clock. *o'clock【əˋklɑk】 副詞 點鐘 現在…點。
答句2	It is + 點 + 分. 現在…點…分。

例句1：

問 What time is it, Susan?

蘇珊，現在幾點？

答 It's seven o'clock

現在七點。

例句2：

問 What time is it, Eileen?

艾琳，現在幾點？

答 It's seven thirty.

現在七點半。

2.

問句	What time + do / does + 主詞 + 原形動詞…?
答句	主詞 + 動詞片詞 + at / before / after + 時間… *before【brˋfor】 介係詞 在…之前 *after【ˋæftɚ】 介係詞 在…之後

例句1：

問 What time do you get up every day?

　你每天幾點起床?

答 I get up at six forty-five every day.

　我每天六點四十五分起床。

例句2：

問 What time does your daughter go to bed every day?

　你女兒每天幾點睡覺?

答 She goes to bed before ten o'clock every day.

　她每天十點前睡覺。

重點二

早上、中午、下午、晚上

1.

> in the + morning / afternoon / evening
>
> 在早上 / 下午 / 晚上
>
> *morning【ˋmɔrnɪŋ】 名詞 早上
>
> *afternoon【ˋæftəˋnun】 名詞 下午
>
> *evening【ˋivnɪŋ】 名詞 傍晚，晚上

2.

> at noon / night / midnight
>
> 在正午 / 夜晚 / 半夜
>
> *noon【nun】 名詞 正午
>
> *night【naɪt】 名詞 夜晚
>
> *midnight【ˋmɪd͵naɪt】 名詞 半夜

例句1：He often works at night.

　　　　他常在晚上工作。

例句2：I usually get up at seven o'clock in the morning.

　　　　我通常早上七點起床。

重點三

星期：(1)要大寫 (2) on + 星期

(一)星期名稱表

星期名稱	中文	音標
Monday	星期一	【`mʌnde】
Tuesday	星期二	【`tjuzde】
Wednesday	星期三	【`wɛnzde】
Thursday	星期四	【`θɝzde】
Friday	星期五	【`fraɪ,de】
Saturday	星期六	【`sætɚde】
Sunday	星期日	【`sʌnde】

(二)詢問星期的句型：

問句	What day is today? 今天星期幾? *day【de】 名詞 日，一天 *today【tə`de】 名詞 今天
答句	It is + 星期.

例句1：

問 What day is today?

今天星期幾?

答 It is Friday.

今天星期五。

例句2：

問 Is the baseball game on Sunday?

棒球賽是在星期日嗎？

答 No, it's on Saturday.

不是，是在星期六。

重點四

月份：(1) 要大寫　(2) in + 月份

(一) 月份名稱表

月份名稱	中文	音標
January	一月	【`dʒænjʊˌɛrɪ】
February	二月	【`fɛbrʊˌɛrɪ】
March	三月	【martʃ】
April	四月	【`eprəl】
May	五月	【me】
June	六月	【dʒun】
July	七月	【dʒu`laɪ】
August	八月	【`ɔgəst】
September	九月	【sɛp`tɛmbɚ】
October	十月	【ak`tobɚ】
November	十一月	【no`vɛmbɚ】
December	十二月	【dɪ`sɛmbɚ】

(二)詢問月份的句型：

問句	What month is it? 現在幾月？ *month【mʌnθ】名詞 月
答句	It's + 月份.

例句1：

問 What month is it?

現在幾月？

答 It's February.

現在是二月。

例句2：

問 When will the new shop(商店) open(開幕)?

這家新店何時開幕？

答 It will open in September.

它將在九月開幕。

重點五

日期：(1) date【det】名詞 日期 (2)會用到「序數」

(一)訊問日期的句型：

問句	What's the date today? 今天幾月幾號？
答句	It's + 月份 + 序數.

問句	What's the date of + the 名詞?
	…是幾月幾日?
答句	It's + on +月份 + 序數.
	…是在…月…日。

例句1：

問 What's the date today?

今天幾月幾號?

答 It's April first.

今天是四月一日。

例句2：

問 What's the date of the exam(考試)?

考試日期是幾月幾日?

答 It's on July second.

是在七月二日。

(二)英文「序數」1～31的寫法

序數	英文寫法	音標
第1	first 或 1st	【fɜst】
第2	second 或 2nd	【ˋsɛkənd】
第3	third 或 3rd	【θɜd】
第4	fourth 或 4th	【forθ】
第5	fifth 或 5th	【fɪfθ】
第6	sixth 或 6th	【sɪksθ】
第7	seventh 或 7th	【ˋsɛvənθ】

第8	eighth 或 8th	【eθ】
第9	ninth 或 9th	【naɪnθ】
第10	tenth 或 10th	【tɛnθ】
第11	eleventh 或 11th	【ɪˋlɛvənθ】
第12	twelfth 或 12th	【twɛlfθ】
第13	thirteenth 或 13th	【ˋθɝˋtinθ】
第14	fourteenth 或 14th	【ˋforˋtinθ】
第15	fifteenth 或 15th	【ˋfɪfˋtinθ】
第16	sixteenth 或 16th	【ˋsɪksˋtinθ】
第17	seventeenth 或 17th	【͵sɛvənˋtinθ】
第18	eighteenth 或 18th	【ˋeˋtinθ】
第19	nineteenth 或 19th	【ˋnaɪnˋtinθ】
第20	twentieth 或 20th	【ˋtwɛntɪɪθ】
第21	twenty-first 或 21st	【͵twɛntɪˋfɝst】
第22	twenty-second 或 22nd	【͵twɛntɪˋsɛkənd】
第23	twenty-third 或 23rd	【͵twɛntɪˋθɝd】
第24	twenty-fourth 或 24th	【͵twɛntɪˋforθ】
第25	twenty-fifth 或 25th	【͵twɛntɪˋfɪfθ】
第26	twenty-sixth 或 26th	【͵twɛntɪˋsɪksθ】
第27	twenty-seventh 或 27th	【͵twɛntɪˋsɛvnθ】
第28	twenty-eighth 或 28th	【͵twɛntɪˋeθ】
第29	twenty-ninth 或 29th	【͵twɛntɪˋnaɪnθ】
第30	thirtieth 或 30th	【ˋθɝtɪɪθ】
第31	thirty-first 或 31st	【͵θɝtɪˋfɝst】

重點六

四季：(1) season 【`sizən】 名詞 季節 (2) in + 四季

(一) 季節名稱表

季節	中文	音標
春	spring	【sprɪŋ】
夏	summer	【`sʌmɚ】
秋	fall或autumn	【fɔl】／【`ɔtəm】
冬	winter	【`wɪntɚ】

(二) 詢問季節的句型：

問句	What season is it now? 現在是什麼季節?
答句	It is + 季節 + now. 現在是…。

例句1：

問 What season is it now?

現在是什麼季節?

答 It is fall now.

現在是秋天。

例句2：

問 How is the weather (天氣) in summer in Taiwan?

台灣夏天的氣候如何?

答 It is hot(炎熱的) in summer in Taiwan.

台灣夏天天氣炎熱。

實際運用短文 ➜ Track 016

Two Wonderful Holidays in Winter

To me, two holidays in winter impress me the most. One is Christmas Day, and the other is New Year Day. The former is on December 25th, and the latter is on January 1st. It is usually very cold during the two holidays because it is in winter in Taiwan. It seldom snows and rains then, so there are many outdoor activities for celebration in December and January. Many people take the MRT to join in the activities then, and it is crowded everywhere. However, the activities and shows are very interesting and wonderful! I always have a good time during the two holidays.

冬天兩個精彩的節日

對我來說，兩個在冬天的節日令我印象最深刻。一個是聖誕節，另一個是新年。前者在十二月二十五日，後者在一月一日。通常在這兩個假期間天氣非常寒冷，因為是台灣的冬天。那時候很少下雪或下雨，所以在十二月跟一月有很多戶外慶祝活動。那時候很多人搭捷運去參加這些活動，到處都是人潮擁擠。然而，活動跟表演非常有趣精彩。這兩個節日我總是過得很開心。

重點註解

Track 016

1. wonderful【`wʌndə·fəl】 形容詞 極好的，精彩的

2. holiday【`hɑlə,de】 名詞 節日，假日

3. one…, and the other… 一個…，另一個…

4. Christmas Day【`krɪsməs】【de】 名詞片語 耶誕節

5. New Year Day【nju】【jɪr】【de】 名詞片語 新年

6. the former【`fɔrmə·】…, and the latter【`lætə·】…
   前者…，後者…

7. cold【kold】 形容詞 寒冷的

8. during【`djurɪŋ】 介係詞 在…期間

9. snow【sno】 動詞 下雪

10. rain【ren】 動詞 下雨

11. then【ðɛn】 副詞 那時

12. outdoor【`aut,dor】 形容詞 戶外的

13. activity【æk`tɪvətɪ】 名詞 活動

14. celebration【,sɛlə`breʃən】 名詞 慶祝

15. join in【dʒɔɪn】【ɪn】+活動 參加…活動

16. crowded【`kraudɪd】 形容詞 擁擠的

17. everywhere【`ɛvrɪ,hwɛr】 副詞 到處

18. show【ʃo】 名詞 表演，秀

19. interesting【`ɪntərɪstɪŋ】 形容詞 有趣的

20. wonderful【`wʌndə·fəl】 形容詞 極好的，精彩的

21. have a good time 動詞片語 玩得很開心

練習題

I. 連貫式翻譯 (一)

1. 我和爸爸都喜歡打籃球。
2. 我們常去運動公園看籃球賽。
3. 七月在運動公園將有兩場籃球賽。
4. 有一場在周五,一場在周日。
5. 兩場都是在下午三點開打。

II. 連貫式翻譯 (二)

1. 母親節在五月的第二個星期日。
2. 我和家人在那一天都會去餐廳慶祝。
3. 今年的母親節在周日,日期是五月十二日。
4. 那天我們打算早上十一點去一家餐廳。
5. 我們將度過美好的時光。

III. 請找出《實際運用短文 - Two Wonderful Holidays in Winter》一文中有運用到本單元教學討論的「時間片語」,並將該部分劃上底線。

解答

I.

| 1 | Both my father and I like to play basketball. |

2	We often go to the sports park to watch basketball games.
3	There will be two basketball games in July.
4	One is on Friday, and the other is on Sunday.
5	Both of them start at three o'clock in the afternoon.

II.

1	Mother's Day is on the second Sunday in May.
2	My family and I always go to a restaurant for celebration on that day.
3	Mother's Day is on Sunday, May 12th this year.
4	We plan to go to a restaurant at eleven o'clock in the morning on that day.
5	We will have a good time.

III.

1. To me, two holidays <u>in winter</u> impress me the most.

2. The former is <u>on December 25th</u>, and the latter is <u>on January 1st</u>.

3. It is usually very cold during the two holidays because it is <u>in winter</u> in Taiwan.

4. It seldom snows and rains then, so there are many outdoor activities for celebration <u>in December</u> and <u>January</u>.

助動詞

重點一

助動詞就是「幫助動詞」的詞類，因為動詞並不能表現所有的動作，在許多的情況下要有助動詞的幫助，否則無法表達出說話者的意思。

例如如果某人想表達：「她可以用我的電腦 = she can use my computer」，如果不用助動詞(can)，就只能表達出 she uses my computer(她使用我的電腦)。只有再加上助動詞can後，才能表達出說話者完整的意思。

重點二

一般而言助動詞有以下幾種：

1. 助動詞(can/must/may/should/shall/do) + 原形動詞→表語氣
   *為本章討論的重點，將就初學者常見的助動詞作介紹。

2. (1) do/does在現在簡單式裡，協助形成「否定句」及「疑問句」(本書第六章已經討論過)

   (2) did在過去簡單式裡，協助形成「否定句」及「疑問句」

   (詳見本書第十一章，將有詳細的說明)

3. (1) 助動詞(have/has) + p.p. →表「現在完成式」

   (詳見本書第十五章，將有詳細的說明)

   (2) 助動詞(had) + p.p. →表「過去完成式」

   (詳見本書第十七章，將有詳細的說明)

4. 助動詞(will) + 原形動詞 →表「未來式」

   (詳見本書第十八章，將有詳細的說明)

重點三

助動詞 (can/must/may/should/shall/do) + 原形動詞
→表語氣

1. can + 原形動詞，表示「能力」= be able to + 原形動詞

例1：Vincent can speak Taiwanese.

= Vincent is able to speak Taiwanese.

文生會說台語。

例2：Vicky can dance well.

= Vicky is able to dance well.

維琪跳舞可以跳得很好。

2. must + 原形動詞，表示「必須」，等於have to + 原形動詞

例1：You must do the homework.

= You have to do the homework.

你必須做家課。

例2：You must tell the truth.

= You have to tell the truth.

你必須說實話。

3. may + 原形動詞，表示「允許」= be allowed to + 原形動詞

例1：You may call him now.

= You are allowed to call him now.

現在你可以打電話給他。

例2：May I talk to you?

= Am I allowed to talk to you?

我可以跟你說話嗎？

英文文法不小心學會了　　139

4. should + 原形動詞，表示「應該」

例1：You should study hard.

你應該用功讀書。

例2：If you meet Helen, you should chat with her.

如果你遇見海倫，你應該跟她聊天。

5. shall

1. 在現代英語中，shall與will的混用十分明顯，不論人稱，will/shall都可表示主詞的「意願」或「單純未來」。

2. 第一人稱用shall/will，第二／三人稱用will

例1：I shall(或will) be twenty next birthday.

我下一次生日就二十歲了。(表主詞的單純未來)

例2：She will not join us.

她不要加入我們。(表主詞的意願)

6. 助動詞 (do/does/did) + 原形動詞

助動詞(do/does/did)用來加強肯定句中動詞的語氣，此時的助動詞(do/does/did)可譯為「的確」。do/does依人稱做變化，用在現在簡單式裡。did用在過去簡單式裡。

例1：He likes her. 他喜歡她。

→He does like her. 他的確喜歡她。

例2：They work hard. 他們工作勤奮。

→They do work hard. 他們的確工作勤奮。

例3：I went to the party last night. 我昨晚去了派對。

→I did go to the party last night. 我昨晚的確有去派對。

Jobs and Dressing Up

There are many different kinds of jobs. When people first get to know you, they may be interested in your job. "What do you do?" is a question for asking about your job. However, sometimes people can just know your job by your look. For example, a nurse or a doctor usually wears white clothes, so if someone wears white clothes all over his or her body, you may think he or she must be a nurse or a doctor. On the other hand, you should know how to dress for your job. Sometimes, dressing well for a job interview can be an important factor for getting the job.

工作和打扮

有很多不同的工作。當人們剛開始認識你時，他們也許會對你的工作感興趣。「你從事什麼工作?」是一個詢問你職業的問題。然而，有時候人們藉著你的外表就可以知道你的工作。舉例來說，護士或醫生通常穿著白衣，所以如果某人全身穿著白衣，你也許會認為他或她一定就是護士或醫生。從另一方面來說，你應該要知道如何依工作而穿著。有時候，工作面試時好的穿著可以是決定錄取與否的重要因素。

重點註解

Track 017

1. different 【`dɪfərənt】 形容詞 不同的

2. kind 【kaɪnd】 名詞 種類

3. job 【dʒɑb】 名詞 工作

4. first 【fɜˑst】 副詞 最初

5. get to + 原形動詞 達到…階段

6. know 【no】 動詞 認識

7. interested 【`ɪntərɪstɪd】 形容詞 感到興趣的
   be interested in + 名詞 / V-ing 對…感到興趣

8. for 【fɔr】 介係詞 為了

9. ask about 【æsk】【ə`baʊt】 動詞片語 詢問

10. just 【dʒʌst】 副詞 僅僅，就…

11. by 【baɪ】 介係詞 藉著，經由

12. look 【lʊk】 名詞 外表，樣子

13. for example 【fɔr】【ɪg`zæmp!】 介係詞片語 舉例來說

14. nurse 【nɜˑs】 名詞 護士

15. doctor 【`dɑktə】 名詞 醫生

16. wear 【wɛr】 動詞 穿

17. white 【hwaɪt】 形容詞 白色的

18. clothes 【kloz】 名詞 衣服

19. someone 【`sʌm,wʌn】 代名詞 某人

20. all over one's body 介係詞片語 遍及全身
    body 【`bɑdɪ】 名詞 身體

21. think【θɪŋk】 **動詞** 想，認為
22. on the other hand **介係詞片語** 另一方面來說
23. how to + 原形動詞　如何去…
24. dress【drɛs】 **動詞** 打扮，穿衣
25. well【wɛl】 **副詞** 很好的，妥善地
26. interview【`ɪntə‚vju】 **名詞** 面試
27. important【ɪm`pɔrtnt】 **形容詞** 重要的
28. factor【`fæktə】 **名詞** 因素
29. get【gɛt】 **動詞** 得到

練習題

I. 連貫式翻譯 (一)

1. 我爸媽認為我應該要用功讀書。
2. 他們認為我必須就讀好的大學。
3. 但是，我或許不是一個好學生。
4. 我的確讀很多書。
5. 但我只讀課外書籍。

II. 連貫式翻譯 (二)

1. 凱莉也許是我們班最受歡迎的同學。
2. 她可以唱歌、跳舞，甚至寫小說。
3. 此外，她可以教她的同學演戲。
4. 我們老師認為她必須進入藝術大學就讀。
5. 我們班同學也認為她應該去當藝人。

英文文法 不小就 學會了

III. 請找出《實際運用短文 - Jobs and Dressing Up》一文中有運用到本單元教學討論的「助動詞+原形動詞」，並將該部分劃上底線。

解答

I.

1	My parents think I should study hard.
2	They think I must enter a good university.
3	However, I may not be a good student.
4	I do read a lot of books.
5	But I only read extracurricular books.

II.

1	Kelly may be the most popular student in our class.
2	She can sing, dance, and even write a novel.
3	Also, she can teach her classmates acting.
4	Our teacher thinks she must enter an art university.
5	Our classmates also think she should be an artist.

III.

1. When people first get to know you, they <u>may be</u> interested in your job.

2. "What <u>do</u> you <u>do</u>?" is a question for asking about your job.

3. However, sometimes people <u>can</u> just <u>know</u> your job by your look.

4. For example, a nurse or a doctor usually wears white clothes, so if someone wears white clothes all over his or her body, you <u>may think</u> he or she <u>must be</u> a nurse or a doctor.

5. On the other hand, you <u>should know</u> how to dress for your job.

6. Sometimes, dressing well for a job interview <u>can be</u> an important factor for getting the job.

英文 **ENGLISH**

GRAMMAR 文法

不小心就 學會了

PART
11

過去簡單式

重點一：be動詞的過去式

(一) be動詞「現在式」與「過去式」對應表

be動詞現在式	音標	be動詞過去式	音標
am	【æm】	was	【wɑz】
is	【ɪz】	was	【wɑz】
are	【ɑr】	were	【wɝ】

(二) 常與「過去時間副詞 (片語)」連用，常見的有：

1. yesterday (昨天), before (以前), just now (剛才)

   *yesterday 【`jɛstɚ.de】 副詞 昨天

   *before 【bɪ`for】 副詞 以前

   *just now 【dʒʌst】【naʊ】 副詞片語 剛才

2. yesterday morning/afternoon/evening 昨天早上/下午/晚上

   *morning 【`mɔrnɪŋ】 名詞 早上

   *afternoon 【`æftɚ`nun】 名詞 下午

   *evening 【`ivnɪŋ】 名詞 傍晚，晚上

3. the day before yesterday 前天

   *before 【bɪ`for】 介係詞 在…之前

4. last night/week/month/year 昨晚/上週/上個月/去年

   *last 【læst】 形容詞 上次的，最近的

   *night 【naɪt】 名詞 夜晚

   *week 【wik】 名詞 週，星期

   *month 【mʌnθ】 名詞 月

   *year 【jɪr】 名詞 年

5. 一段時間 + ago

 *ago【əˋgo】**副詞** 在…以前

例1：She was sick <u>yesterday</u>.

  她昨天生病。

例2：David was a magician <u>before</u>.

  大衛以前是魔術師。

例3：My parents were home <u>last night</u>.

  我父母昨晚在家。

例4：We were busy <u>last month</u>.

  上個月我們很忙。

例5：My mother went shopping <u>yesterday afternoon</u>.

  我媽媽昨天下午去購物。

例6：I went to Taipei <u>three days ago</u>.

  三天前我去台北。

重點二：一般動詞的過去式

1. 規則變化：字尾加d、ed、去y加ied，或重複字尾再加
 上ed，常見的如下表：

一般動詞 （原形）	過去式 （字尾加d）	中文意思	過去式動詞 的音標
close	closed	關上	【klozd】
move	moved	移動，搬家	【muvd】
like	liked	喜歡	【laɪkt】
use	used	使用	【juzd】

一般動詞 （原形）	過去式 （字尾加ed）	中文意思	過去式動詞 的音標
open	opened	打開	【ˋopənd】
play	played	玩	【pled】
talk	talked	說話	【tɔkt】
ask	asked	問	【æskt】
jump	jumped	跳	【dʒʌmpt】
wash	washed	洗	【waʃt】
call	called	打電話，稱呼	【kɔld】
listen	listened	聽	【ˋlɪsənd】
watch	watched	觀看	【watʃt】

一般動詞 （原形）	過去式 （字尾加ied） 【註解：動詞字尾是「子音+y」時，須先去掉y，再加ied】	中文意思	過去式動詞 的音標
fly	flied	飛	【flaɪd】
study	studied	學習，研究	【ˋstʌdɪd】
try	tried	嘗試	【traɪd】

一般動詞 (原形)	過去式 (重複字尾加ed) 【註解：動詞字尾呈「子音＋母音＋子音」排列時，則須重覆字尾，再加ed】	中文意思	過去式動詞 的音標
drop	dropped	滴下，掉下	【drɑpt】
jog	jogged	慢跑	【dʒɑgd】
stop	stopped	停止	【stɑpt】

2. 不規則變化：只能背熟，看到一個就記一個。

　　常見的如下表：

原形動詞	音標	過去式	音標
buy(買)	【baɪ】	bought	【bɔt】
come(來)	【kʌm】	came	【kem】
do(做)	【du】	did	【dɪd】
go(去)	【go】	went	【wɛnt】
give(給)	【gɪv】	gave	【gev】
make(製造)	【mek】	made	【mod】
read(閱讀；看書)	【rid】	read	【rɛd】
run(跑)	【rʌn】	ran	【ræn】
see(看；看見)	【si】	saw	【sɔ】
sit(坐)	【sɪt】	sat	【sæt】

speak(説)	【spik】	spoke	【spok】
teach(教；教書)	【titʃ】	taught	【tɔt】

原形動詞	音標	過去式	音標
wear(穿)	【wɛr】	wore	【wor】
hear(聽)	【hɪr】	heard	【hɝd】
catch(抓；捉)	【kætʃ】	caught	【kɔt】
drink(喝)	【drɪŋk】	drank	【dræŋk】
eat(吃)	【it】	ate	【et】
find(發現；找到)	【faɪnd】	found	【faʊnd】
get(獲得)	【gɛt】	got	【gɑt】
have(有；吃；喝)	【hæv】	had	【hæd】
put(放置)	【pʊt】	put	【pʊt】
ride(騎)	【raɪd】	rode	【rod】
say(説)	【se】	said	【sɛd】
sing(唱；唱歌)	【sɪŋ】	sang	【sæŋ】
sleep(睡覺)	【slip】	slept	【slɛpt】
stand(站立)	【stænd】	stood	【stʊd】
take(拿；搭乘)	【tek】	took	【tʊk】
write(寫)	【raɪt】	wrote	【rot】
forget(忘記)	【fɚˋgɛt】	forgot	【fɚˋgɑt】
grow(成長；種植)	【gro】	grew	【gru】
pay(付錢)	【pe】	paid	【ped】

重點三：過去簡單式的否定句

(一) 過去式be動詞 + not = 否定句 =「不是」

  *was not可縮寫成wasn't【`wɑzənt】

  *were not可縮寫成weren't【wɝnt】

(二) 主詞 + didn't + 原形動詞…

  *didn't【`dɪdənt】= did not

  → did為助動詞do的過去式，在此的功用為協助一般動詞「造否定句」。

例1：It <u>was not</u> cold yesterday. It was hot.

  昨天天氣不冷。天氣炎熱。

例2：They <u>were not</u> in Taipei last year. They were in Kaohsiung.

  去年他們不在台北。他們在高雄。

例3：I <u>didn't play</u> basketball last month.

  上個月我沒有打籃球。

例4：Lisa <u>didn't clean</u> her room last week.

  麗莎上個禮拜沒有打掃房間。

重點四：過去簡單式的疑問句

(一) 有過去式be動詞的句子

1. 將「主詞 + 過去式be動詞」改為「過去式be動詞 + 主詞…?」要記得將句尾改成問號「?」

例句1：

肯定句 Lession Six was difficult.

第六課很難。

疑問句 <u>Was Lession Six</u> difficult?

第六課很難嗎？

例句2：

肯定句 They were fat three years ago.

三年前他們很胖。

疑問句 <u>Were they</u> fat three years ago?

三年前他們很胖嗎？

2. 回答時，可用簡答或詳答的方式：

(1) 肯定簡答：Yes, 代名詞 + 過去式be動詞.

　　肯定詳答：Yes, (代名詞 + 過去式be動詞.) + 句子.

例句1：Was his wife a teacher before?

　　　他老婆以前是老師嗎？

簡答 Yes, she was.

　　是的，她是。

詳答 Yes, she was. She was a teacher before.

　　是的，她是。她以前是老師。

詳答 Yes, she was a teacher before.

　　是的，她以前是老師。

例句2： Were they students two years ago?

　　　　兩年前他們是學生嗎？

簡答　Yes, they were.

　　　　是的，他們是。

詳答　Yes, they were. They were students two years ago.

　　　　是的，他們是。他們兩年前是學生。

詳答　Yes, they were students two years ago.

　　　　是的，他們兩年前是學生。

(2)否定簡答：No, 代名詞＋過去式be動詞＋not(可用縮寫體).

　　否定詳答：No,〔代名詞＋過去式be動詞＋not(可用縮寫體).〕

　　　　　　　　＋否定句子.

例句1： Was his wife a teacher before?

　　　　他老婆以前是老師嗎？

簡答　No, she was not.(或No, she wasn't.)

　　　　不，她不是。

詳答　No, she was not.(或No, she wasn't.) She was not a
teacher before.

　　　　不，她不是。她以前不是老師。

詳答　No, she was not(或wasn't) a teacher before.

　　　　不，她以前不是老師。

例句2： Were they students two years ago?

　　　　兩年前他們是學生嗎？

簡答　No, they were not.(或No, they weren't.)

　　　　不，他們不是。

詳答 No, they were not. (或No, they weren't.) They were

not students two years ago.

不，他們不是。他們兩年前不是學生。

詳答 No, they were not(或weren't) students two years ago.

不，他們兩年前不是學生。

(二)有一般動詞的句子

1. Did + 主詞 + 原形動詞…?

*did為助動詞do的過去式，在此的功用為協助一般動詞

「造疑問句」。

例句1：

肯定句 Mary met him in the park last week.

瑪莉上週在公園遇見他。

疑問句 <u>Did Mary meet</u> him in the park last week?

瑪莉上週在公園遇見他嗎？

例句2：

肯定句 You went to the concert yesterday.

你昨天去音樂會。

疑問句 <u>Did you go</u> to the concert yesterday?

你昨天有去音樂會嗎？

2. 回答時，可用簡答或詳答的方式：

(1)肯定簡答：Yes, 代名詞 + did.

肯定詳答：Yes, (代名詞 + did.) + 句子.

例句：<u>Did Mary meet</u> him in the park last week?

瑪莉上週在公園遇見他嗎？

簡答 Yes, she did.

是的，她是。

詳答 Yes, she did. She met him in the park last week.

是的，她是。她上週在公園遇見他。

詳答 Yes, she met him in the park last week.

是的，她上週在公園遇見他。

(2) 否定簡答：No, 代名詞 + did + not(可用縮寫體).

否定詳答：No,〔代名詞 + did + not(可用縮寫體).〕

+ 否定句子.

例句：<u>Did you go</u> to the concert yesterday?

你昨天有去音樂會嗎？

簡答 No, I did not.(或No, I didn't.)

不，我沒有。

詳答 No, I did not.(或No, I didn't.) I didn't go to the concert yesterday.

不，我沒有。我昨天沒有去音樂會。

詳答 No, I didn't go to the concert yesterday.

不，我昨天沒有去音樂會。

My Birthday Last Year

My birthday last year is unforgettable. I was born on September 8th. My friends and family held a party for me on that day last year in my house. They prepared a lot of foods and drinks. And they even invited my favorite teacher to the party. Moreover, some of my friends enjoyed performing my favorite English songs, and I really enjoyed their performance. We all had a good time together. And I was very happy and cried tears of joy at the end of the party.

我去年的生日

我去年的生日令人難忘。我出生於九月八日。我朋友和家人去年在那一天在我家替我舉行了生日派對。他們準備了很多食物和飲料。他們甚至邀請我最喜歡的老師來。而且我的一些朋友還表演了我最喜歡的英文歌曲，我真的很喜愛他們的表演。我們一起度過了美好的時光。我非常開心，在派對結束時喜極而泣。

1. birthday【`bɝθ,de】名詞 生日

2. last year 時間片語 去年

3. unforgettable【ˌʌnfə`gɛtəbl】形容詞 難忘的

4. born【bɔrn】形容詞 出生的

5. September【sɛp`tɛmbə】名詞 九月

6. hold【hold】動詞 舉行 (過去式held)

7. party【`pɑrtɪ】名詞 宴會，派對

8. for【fɔr】介係詞 替…，為了…

9. on that day 時間片語 那一天

10. in【ɪn】介係詞 在…之內

11. house【haʊs】名詞 房子

12. prepare【prɪ`pɛr】動詞 準備 (過去式prepared)

13. a lot of 形容詞片語 很多…

14. food【fud】名詞 食物

15. drink【drɪŋk】名詞 飲料

16. even【`ivən】副詞 甚至

17. invite【ɪn`vaɪt】動詞 邀請

18. favorite【`fevərɪt】形容詞 最喜歡的

19. moreover【mor`ovə】副詞 此外

20. some of ＋名詞片語 ……中的一些

21. perform【pə`fɔrm】動詞 表演

22. song【sɔŋ】名詞 歌

23. really 【`rɪəlɪ】 副詞 真地

24. enjoy 【ɪn`dʒɔɪ】 動詞 享受，喜愛

25. performance 【pɚ`fɔrməns】 名詞 表演

26. all 【ɔl】 代名詞 全體

27. have a good time 動詞片語 玩得很開心

28. together 【tə`gɛðɚ】 副詞 一起

29. happy 【`hæpɪ】 形容詞 快樂的

30. cry tears of joy 動詞片語 喜極而泣

　　cry 【kraɪ】 動詞 哭(過去式cried)

　　tear 【tɪr】 名詞 眼淚

　　joy 【dʒɔɪ】 名詞 喜悅

31. at the end of ＋ 名詞片語　在…的末端，在…的結束之時

練習題

I. 連貫式翻譯 (一)

1. 我母親生於1月17日。今年60歲。

2. 她以前是個護士。

3. 去年3月她從一家醫院退休。

4. 我們在3月底時替她舉行了慶祝派對。

5. 那天她非常開心。

II. 連貫式翻譯 (二)

1. 大衛以前是個籃球員。

2. 放學後常和同學一起練習籃球。

3. 三年前他從學校畢業。

4. 畢業後，他在電腦公司工作。

5. 因為工作太忙，去年一整年他都沒有打籃球。

III. 請找出《實際運用短文 - My Birthday Last Year》一文中有運用到本單元教學討論的「過去式」的句型，並將該部分劃上底線。

解答

I.

1	My mother was born on January 1st. She is sixty years old now.
2	She was a nurse before.
3	She retired from a hospital last March.
4	We held a celebration party for her at the end of last March.
5	She was very happy on that day. (或She had a good time on that day.)

II.

1	David was a basketball player before.

2	He often practiced basketball with his classmates after school.
3	He graduated from school three years ago.
4	After graduation, he worked in a computer company.
5	Because he was too busy with his work, he didn't play basketball the whole year last year.

III.

1. I was born on September 8th.

2. My friends and family held a birthday party for me on that day last year in my house.

3. They prepared a lot of foods and drinks.

4. And they even invited my favorite teacher to the party.

5. Moreover, some of my friends enjoyed performing my favorite English songs, and I really enjoyed their performance.

6. We all had a good time together.

7. And I was very happy and cried tears of joy at the end of the party.

PART 12

形容詞、
形容詞子句

重點一：形容詞的位置

1. 形容詞 + 名詞（用來修飾名詞）

例1：Kelly is a <u>beautiful girl</u>.

　　凱莉是一個美麗的女孩。

　　*beautiful【`bjutəfəl】 形容詞 美麗的，放在名詞girl前
　　　面，修飾該名詞。

例2：This is a <u>white dog</u>.

　　這是一隻白色的狗。

　　*white【hwaɪt】 形容詞 白色的，放在名詞dog前面，
　　　修飾該名詞。

2. 主詞 + be動詞 + 形容詞（用來說明主詞的狀態）

例1：My younger brother <u>is handsome</u>.

　　我弟弟很帥。

　　*handsome【`hænsəm】 形容詞 英俊的，放在be動詞
　　　(is)後面，當主詞補語，補充說明主詞my younger
　　　brother的狀態。

例2：The vase <u>is pretty</u>.

　　這花瓶很漂亮。

　　*pretty【`prɪtɪ】 形容詞 漂亮的，放在be動詞(is)後
　　　面，當主詞補語，補充說明主詞the vase的狀態。

重點二：形容詞的比較級及最高級

一、動詞有三態，形容詞也有三級：原級、比較級、最高級。

1. 規則變化：

(1) 短字 + er/est

形容詞原級	形容詞比較級	形容詞最高級
*單音節的字在字尾加er及est		
tall (高的)	taller	tallest
long (長的)	longer	longest
clean (乾淨的)	cleaner	cleanest
warm (溫暖的)	warmer	warmest
high (高的)	higher	highest
dark (黑暗的)	darker	darkest
*字尾有e時，只加r及st		
nice (好的)	nicer	nicest
close (近的)	closer	closest
cute (可愛的)	cuter	cutest
wide (寬的)	wider	widest
safe (安全的)	safer	safest
gentle (溫和的)	gentler	gentlest

形容詞原級	形容詞比較級	形容詞最高級
*字尾為子音+y時，將 y 改為 i 再加 er 及 est (注意：母音+y 時，直接加 er 及 est。例如: gray-grayer-grayest)		
happy(快樂的)	happier	happiest
pretty(漂亮的)	prettier	prettiest
dirty(骯髒的)	dirtier	dirtiest
heavy(重的)	heavier	heaviest
noisy(吵鬧的)	noisier	noisiest
easy(容易的)	easier	easiest
*字尾為「短母音＋子音」，重複字尾再加 er 及 est		
big(大的)	bigger	biggest
fat(胖的)	fatter	fattest
red(紅色的)	redder	reddest
hot(熱的)	hotter	hottest
thin(瘦的)	thinner	thinnest
sad(悲傷的)	sadder	saddest
glad(高興的)	gladder	gladdest

(2) more / most + 長字

形容詞原級	形容詞比較級	形容詞最高級
*三音節以上的字及大多數二音節字，特別由 -ful、-less、-able、-ive、-ing 結尾的字		
beautiful(美麗的)	more beautiful	most beautiful
active(活躍的)	more active	most active
interesting(有趣的)	more interesting	most interesting

| useless (無用的) | more useless | most useless |
| durable (持久的) | more durable | most durable |

(3) 有些形容詞可以加er及est或前面加上more / most來形成
比較級和最高級：

形容詞原級	形容詞比較級	形容詞最高級
polite (有禮貌的)	politer或 more polite	politest或 most polite
quiet (安靜的)	quieter或 more quiet	quietest或 most quiet
common (普遍的)	commoner或 more common	commonest或 most common
pleasant (愉悅的)	pleasanter或 more pleasant	pleasantest或 most pleasant

2. 不規則變化：

形容詞原級	形容詞比較級	形容詞最高級
good (好的)	better	best
well (好的，健康的)	better	best
bad (壞的)	worse	worst
many (許多的)	morc	most
much (許多的)	more	most
little (少的，不多的)	less	least

重點三

比較級句型：兩者之間做比較時

1. A + be動詞 / 一般動詞 + 形容詞比較級 + (名詞)
   + than + B　【A比B…】

例1：A basketball is <u>bigger</u> than a baseball.
　　　籃球比棒球大。

例2：John is <u>taller</u> than Tom.
　　　約翰比湯姆高。

例3：For me, English is <u>more interesting</u> than Spanish.
　　　對我來說，英文比西班牙文有趣。

例4：I have <u>more books</u> than you.
　　　我擁有的書比你多。

例5：Julia looks <u>happier</u> than Judy.
　　　茱麗葉看起來比茱蒂開心。

2. A + be動詞 / 一般動詞 + less + 形容詞原級 + (名詞)
   + than + B　【A比B…】

例1：This movie is <u>less exciting</u> than that one.
　　　這部電影比那部電影無聊。

例2：This book is <u>less expensive</u> than that one.
　　　這本書比那本書便宜。

例3：Mark is <u>less tall</u> than Bill.
　　　馬克比比爾矮。

例4：The movie sounds <u>less interesting</u> than that one.

這部電影聽起來比那部無趣。

例5：He has <u>less foreign friends</u> than me.

他的外國朋友比我少。

重點四

最高級句型：二者以上做比較時

1. the + 最高級形容詞

2. 主詞 + be動詞 + the + 最高級形容詞 (+名詞) +

介係詞片語 【主詞是最…】

例1：Luna is <u>the thinnest</u> student in the class.

露那是班上最瘦的學生。

例2：Kevin is <u>the most handsome</u> student in the class.

凱文是班上最英俊的學生。

例3：I am <u>the tallest</u> in my family.

我是我家最高的。

3. 主詞 + be動詞 + the + least + 形容詞原級 (+名詞)

+ 介係詞片語 【主詞是最不…】

例1：My husband is <u>the least interesting</u> man in the world.

我先生是世上最無趣的男人。

例2：This is <u>the least harmful</u>(有害的) product in the category.

這是目錄裡最無害的產品。

英文文法 _{不小心}學會了　　169

重點五

形容詞子句：由關係代名詞所引導，功用是「做形容詞」，以用來修飾「前面的名詞」。

1. 關係代名詞

關係代名詞所代替的名詞稱為「先行詞」，會因其所代替的名詞是人，事，物而有所改變。

2. 名詞(先行詞) + 形容詞子句(=關係代名詞引導的子句)

先行詞 ＼ 關係代名詞	主格	所有格	受格
人	who	whose	whom
物	which	whose	which
人或物	that	whose	that

(1)在形容詞子句中的關係代名詞如果「作主詞」，則用『主格』。

例1： The students <u>who are in her class</u> come from Taipei.

她班上的學生來台北。

　　*解析：who為關係代名詞主格(這裡也可以用that)，代替先行詞 students，並引導形容詞子句who are in her class，以修飾先行詞 students，在其引導的形容詞子句裡作主詞。

例2： The river <u>which flows through the city</u> is beautiful.

流過這城市的河流真是美。

　　*解析：which為關係代名詞主格(這裡也可以用that)，代替先行詞 river，並引導形容詞子句which flows through the city，以修飾先行

詞river，在其引導的形容詞子句裡作主詞，故主詞為單數，動詞 flow因此要加s。

(2) 在形容詞子句中的關係代名詞如果「後面接名詞」，則用『所有格』。

例1：The woman <u>whose hair is brown</u> is her mother.
　　棕色頭髮的婦女是她母親。

　　*解析：whose為關係代名詞所有格，後接名詞hair，並引導形容詞子句 whose hair is brown，以修飾先行詞woman。

例2：The man <u>whose dog keeps barking</u> is my neighbor.
　　那隻一直吠叫的狗的主人是我的鄰居。

　　*解析：whose為關係代名詞所有格，後接名詞dog，並引導形容詞子句 whose dog keeps barking，以修飾先行詞man。

(3) 在形容詞子句中的關係代名詞如果作受詞，則用受格。

例1：The girl <u>whom I met yesterday</u> was friendly.
　　昨天我遇到的那個女孩很友善。

　　*解析：whom為關係代名詞受格(這裡也可以用that)，代替先行詞 girl，並引導形容詞子句 whom I met yesterday，以修飾先行詞girl，在其引導的形容詞子句裡作動詞met的受詞。

例2：He found the key <u>which you lost last night</u>.
　　他找到昨晚你遺失的鑰匙。

　　*解析：which為關係代名詞受格(這裡也可以用that)，代替先行詞 key，並引導形容詞子句 which you lost last night，以修飾先行詞 key，在其引導的形容詞子句裡作動詞lost的受詞。

英文文法秒學會了　　171

Track 019

Leehom Wang's Music

Do you like pop music? For me, pop music is more interesting than classical. I like pop music most because I like to sing. Among the pop music singers, I like Leehom Wang most, for his music is both elegant and powerful. The lyrics and melodies of his songs are touching. Besides, Leehom Wang is tall and handsome. He can play many musical instruments. When you watch him perform on the stage, you may have the most wonderful experience in the pop music world.

王力宏的音樂

你喜歡流行音樂嗎? 對我來說,流行音樂比古典音樂有趣。我最喜歡流行音樂因為我喜歡唱歌。在流行音樂的歌手中,我最喜歡王力宏,因為他的音樂既優雅又強而有力。他歌曲的歌詞和旋律很感人。此外,王力宏高大又帥。他可以彈奏很多樂器。當你觀賞他在舞台上演出的時候,你也許會有在流行音樂世界裡最美好的經歷。

重點註解 ⟶ Track 019

1. pop【pɑp】 形容詞 通俗的，流行的

2. for【fɔr】 介係詞 對…而言

3. interesting【ˋɪntərɪstɪŋ】 形容詞 有趣的

4. classical【ˋklæsɪk!】 形容詞 古典的

5. one【wʌn】 代名詞 代替上文中的名詞或名詞片語。在此代替music。

6. most【most】 副詞最高級 最

7. among【əˋmʌŋ】 介係詞 在…之中

8. singer【ˋsɪŋə】 名詞 歌手

9. 句子, for 句子. for當對等連接詞，意思為「因為」。

10. elegant【ˋɛləgənt】 形容詞 優雅的

11. powerful【ˋpauəfəl】 形容詞 強而有力的

12. lyric【ˋlɪrɪk】 名詞 歌詞

13. melody【ˋmɛlədɪ】 名詞 旋律

14. touching【ˋtʌtʃɪŋ】 形容詞 動人的

15. besides【bɪˋsaɪdz】 副詞 此外

16. tall【tɔl】 形容詞 高大的

17. handsome【ˋhænsəm】 形容詞 英俊的

18. play【ple】 動詞 彈奏

19. musical instrument【ˋmjuzɪk!】【ˋɪnstrəmənt】
    名詞片語 樂器

20. watch【wɑtʃ】 動詞 觀看

英文文法 不小心就 學會了 173

21. perform【pə`fɔrm】 動詞 表演

22. stage【stedʒ】 名詞 舞台

23. wonderful【`wʌndəfəl】 形容詞 奇妙的，極好的

24. experience【ɪk`spɪrɪəns】 名詞 經驗，體驗

25. world【wɜld】 名詞 世界

練習題

I. 連貫式翻譯(一)

1. 那個正在跟我哥說話的男生是一位籃球員。

2. 他很高又壯。

3. 他的手很大，腿很長。

4. 他是今年的最佳球員。

5. 他所待的球隊是台北市裡面最有名的。

II. 連貫式翻譯(二)

1. 丹尼最喜歡的課外活動是跳舞。

2. 他覺得跳舞很有趣，令人放鬆。

3. 下課後和朋友跳舞是他一天中最開心的時刻。

4. 對丹尼來說，運動公園是跳舞最好的場地。

5. 跳舞對他來說比念書還要重要。

III. 請找出《實際運用短文 - Leehom Wang's Music》一文中有運用到本單元教學討論的「形容詞原級、比較級、最高級」的片語或句型，並將該部分劃上底線。

解答

I.

1	The man who (或 that) is talking to my older brother is a basketball player.
2	He is very tall and strong.
3	His hands are very big, and his legs are very long.
4	He is the best player this year.
5	The team which (或 that) he belongs to is the most famous one in Taipei.

II.

1	Danny's favorite extracurricular activity is dancing.
2	He feels dancing is interesting and relaxing.
3	For him, dancing with his friends after school is the happiest time in a day.
4	For Danny, a sports park is the best place to dance.
5	For him, dancing is more important than studying.

III.

1. Do you like <u>pop music</u>?

2. For me, <u>pop music</u> is <u>more interesting</u> than <u>classical</u>.

3. I like <u>pop music</u> most because I like to sing.

4. Among the <u>pop music singers</u>, I like Leehom Wang most, for his music <u>is</u> both <u>elegant</u> and <u>powerful</u>.

5. The lyrics and melodies of his songs <u>are touching</u>.

6. Besides, Leehom Wang <u>is tall</u> and <u>handsome</u>.

7. He can play <u>many musical instruments</u>.

8. When you watch him perform on the stage, you may have <u>the most wonderful experience</u> in the <u>pop music world</u>.

現在分詞和
過去分詞

重點一：現在分詞（V-ing）

(一)使用時機：

「現在分詞」，與 be 搭配(即 be + V-ing)，用於「進行式」
中，在本書後面幾個章節將有詳盡的介紹(現在進行式，過去
進行式)。

(二)現在分詞(V-ing)，常見的如下：

1. 直接在「動詞」的字尾加上ing：

一般動詞 （原形）	字尾加ing （現在分詞）	中文意思	現在分詞的 音標
open	opening	打開	【`opənɪŋ】
play	playing	玩	【`pleɪŋ】
talk	talking	說話	【`tɔkɪŋ】
ask	asking	問	【`æskɪŋ】
jump	jumping	跳	【`dʒʌmpɪŋ】
wash	washing	洗	【`waʃɪŋ】
call	calling	打電話，稱呼	【`kɔlɪŋ】
listen	listening	聽	【`lɪsənɪŋ】
watch	watching	觀看	【`watʃɪŋ】
fly	flying	飛	【`flaɪɪŋ】
study	studying	學習，研究	【`stʌdɪɪŋ】
try	trying	嘗試	【`traɪɪŋ】

2. 若原「動詞」的字尾有不發音的e時，則先去掉字尾e，再加ing：

一般動詞 （原形）	去掉字尾e 再加ing （現在分詞）	中文意思	現在分詞的 音標
close	closing	關上	【 `klozɪŋ 】
move	moving	移動，搬家	【 `muvɪŋ 】
like	liking	喜歡	【 `laɪkɪŋ 】
use	using	使用	【 `juzɪŋ 】

3. 動詞字尾呈「子音＋母音＋子音」排列時，則須重覆字尾，再加ing。

一般動詞 （原形）	重覆字尾 再加ing （現在分詞）	中文意思	現在分詞的 音標
drop	dropping	滴下，掉下	【 `drɑpɪŋ 】
jog	jogging	慢跑	【 `dʒɑgɪŋ 】
stop	stopping	停止	【 `stɑpɪŋ 】
put	putting	放置	【 `pʊtɪŋ 】

重點二：過去分詞 (p.p.)

（一）使用時機：

「過去分詞」主要是用於「完成式」和「被動態」中，在本書後面幾個章節將有詳盡的介紹。

(二)過去分詞(p.p.)為動詞三態變化中的「第三態」，常見
  的如下：

1. 規則變化：字尾加d、ed、去y加ied，或重複字尾再加上ed。

一般動詞 (原形)	過去式 (字尾加d)	過去分詞 (字尾加d) (p.p.)	中文意思	過去分詞 (p.p.) 的音標
第一態	第二態	第三態		
close	closed	closed	關上	【klozd】
move	moved	moved	移動，搬家	【muvd】
like	liked	liked	喜歡	【laɪkt】
use	used	used	使用	【juzd】

一般動詞 (原形)	過去式 (字尾加ed)	過去分詞 (字尾加ed) (p.p.)	中文意思	過去分詞 (p.p.) 的音標
open	opened	opened	打開	【`opənd】
play	played	played	玩	【pled】
talk	talked	talked	說話	【tɔkt】
ask	asked	asked	問	【æskt】
jump	jumped	jumped	跳	【dʒʌmpt】
wash	washed	washed	洗	【wɑʃt】
call	called	called	打電話，稱呼	【kɔld】

| listen | listened | listened | 聽 | 【`lɪsənd】 |
| watch | watched | watched | 觀看 | 【watʃt】 |

一般動詞 (原形)	過去式 (字尾加ied) 【註解：動詞字尾是「子音＋y」時，須先去掉y，再加ied】	過去分詞 (字尾加ied) (p.p.)	中文意思	過去分詞 (p.p.)的音標
fly	flied	flied	飛	【flaɪd】
study	studied	studied	學習，研究	【`stʌdɪd】
try	tried	tried	嘗試	【traɪd】

一般動詞 (原形)	過去式(重覆字尾，再加上ed) 【註解：動詞字尾呈「子音＋母音＋子音」排列時，則須重覆字尾，再加ed】	過去分詞 (重覆字尾再加上ed) (p.p.)	中文意思	過去分詞 (p.p.)的音標
drop	dropped	dropped	滴下，掉下	【drapt】
jog	jogged	jogged	慢跑	【dʒagd】
stop	stopped	stopped	停止	【stapt】

2. 不規則變化：只能背熟，看到一個就記一個。更好的方法是「從文章中」去熟悉這些不規則過去式動詞及過去分詞 (p.p)。常見的如下表：

一般動詞(原形)	過去式	過去分詞(p.p.)
第一態	第二態	第三態
buy(買)【baɪ】	bought【bɔt】	bought【bɔt】
come(來)【kʌm】	came【kem】	come【kʌm】
do(做)【du】	did【dɪd】	done【dʌn】
go(去)【go】	went【wɛnt】	gone【gɔn】
give(給)【gɪv】	gave【gev】	given【`gɪvən】
make(製造)【mek】	made【med】	made【med】
read(閱讀；看書)【rid】	read【rɛd】	read【rɛd】
run(跑)【rʌn】	ran【ræn】	run【rʌn】
see(看；看見)【si】	saw【sɔ】	seen【sin】
sit(坐)【sɪt】	sat【sæt】	sat【sæt】
speak(説)【spik】	spoke【spok】	spoken【`spokən】
teach(教；教書)【titʃ】	taught【tɔt】	taught【tɔt】
wear(穿)【wɛr】	wore【wor】	worn【worn】
hear(聽)【hɪr】	heard【hɝd】	heard【hɝd】
catch(抓；捉)【kætʃ】	caught【kɔt】	caught【kɔt】
drink(喝)【drɪŋk】	drank【dræŋk】	drunk【drʌŋk】
eat(吃)【it】	ate【el】	caten【`itən】
find(發現；找到)【faɪnd】	found【faʊnd】	found【faʊnd】
get(獲得)【gɛt】	got【gɑt】	got【gɑt】或 gotten【`gɑtən】

have(有;吃;喝)【hæv】	had【hæd】	had【hæd】
put(放置)【pʊt】	put【pʊt】	put【pʊt】
ride(騎)【raɪd】	rode【rod】	ridden【`rɪdən】
say(說)【se】	said【sɛd】	said【sɛd】
sell(賣)【sɛl】	sold【sold】	sold【sold】
sing(唱;唱歌)【sɪŋ】	sang【sæŋ】	sung【sʌŋ】
sleep(睡覺)【slip】	slept【slɛpt】	slept【slɛpt】
stand(站立)【stænd】	stood【stʊd】	stood【stʊd】
take(拿;搭乘)【tek】	took【tʊk】	taken【`tekən】
write(寫)【raɪt】	wrote【rot】	written【`rɪtən】
forget(忘記)【fə`gɛt】	forgot【fə`gat】	forgot【fə`gat】 或 forgotten【fə`gatən】
grow(成長;種植)【gro】	grew【gru】	grown【gron】
pay(付錢)【pe】	paid【ped】	paid【ped】

重點三

現在分詞和過去分詞可當「形容詞」用：

*可分兩種：

1. 一般動詞而來：Ving(主動) / p.p.(被動)

2. 情緒動詞而來：Ving(令人感到…的) /

   　　　　　　　p.p.(感到…的)

(一)「一般動詞」而來的現在分詞和過去分詞當形容詞用

1. 現在分詞(V-ing) + 名詞

   *現在分詞(V-ing)表主動

2. 過去分詞(p.p.) + 名詞

　*過去分詞(p.p.)表被動

例1：The <u>barking</u> dog is fierce.

那隻吠叫的狗很兇猛。

　*解析：barking為動詞bark的現在分詞，當形容詞用，修飾dog。

　　狗「主動」做吠叫的動作。

例2：The <u>broken</u> vase is expensive.

這破損的花瓶很貴。

　*解析：broken為動詞break的過去分詞，當形容詞用，修飾vase。

　　花瓶是「被」打破的。

(二)「情緒動詞」而來的現在分詞和過去分詞當形容詞用

1. 常見的情緒動詞如下表：

情緒動詞(原形)	現在分詞(V-ing)	過去分詞(p.p.)
surprise(驚訝)	surprising【sə`praɪzɪŋ】	surprised【sə`praɪzd】
confuse(困惑)	confusing【kən`fjuzɪŋ】	confused【kən`fjuzd】
excite(興奮)	exciting【ɪk`saɪtɪŋ】	excited【ɪk`saɪtɪd】
bore(無聊)	boring【`borɪŋ】	bored【bord】
interest(興趣)	interesting【`ɪntərɪstɪŋ】	interested【`ɪntərɪstɪd】

2. 情緒動詞的現在分詞(V-ing)修飾「事物」，意思為「令人感
　到…」。情緒動詞的過去分詞(p.p.)修飾「人」，意思為「感到
　…」。

例1：This in an <u>interesting</u> book. 這是一本有趣的書。

　*解析：interesting為情緒動詞interest的現在分詞，當形容詞用，修

　　飾book(事物)，意思是「令人感到有趣的」。

例2：I am <u>interested</u> in Japanese. 我對日文感興趣。

*解析：interested為情緒動詞interest的過去分詞，當形容詞用，修

飾 I (人)，意思是「感到興趣的」。

實際運用短文 ➡  Track 020

Kelly's Music Life

　　Kelly works in a music company. She usually has to work from 9:00 a.m. to 11:00 p.m. on weekdays. Sometimes she feels really exhausted, but most of the time she feels her job is very interesting and exciting. For one thing, she can see many artists that appear in her company. For another, she likes music so much that she can't bear a boring life without music. For her, music is a deciding factor in choosing a job. Without music, life may be broken for her.

凱莉的音樂生活

　　凱莉在音樂公司上班。在平常日時，她平日通常必須從早上九點工作到晚上十一點。有時候她覺得真的很疲憊，但大多數的時候她覺得她的工作是很有趣及刺激的。一來，她可以看到很多出現在她公司的藝人。二來她是如此喜歡音樂，以致於她無法忍受沒有音樂的無聊生活。對她而言，音樂是選擇工作時的決定性因素。沒有音樂，生活對她而言是破碎的。

1. company【ˋkʌmpənɪ】 名詞 公司

2. has to + 原形動詞　必須…

3. a.m.　上午 (= before noon)

4. p.m.　下午，午後 (= post meridiem)

5. weekday【ˋwik͵de】 名詞 平日，工作日

6. really【ˋrɪəlɪ】 副詞 真地

7. exhausted【ɪgˋzɔstɪd】 形容詞 筋疲力盡的
   *由動詞 exhaust【ɪgˋzɔst】(用完，耗盡)，所變化而來。

8. most of the time　時間片語 大多數的時候

9. interesting【ˋɪntərɪstɪŋ】 形容詞 有趣的
   *由動詞 interest【ˋɪntərɪst】(使發生興趣)，所變化而來。

10. exciting【ɪkˋsaɪtɪŋ】 形容詞 令人興奮的，刺激的
    *由動詞 excite【ɪkˋsaɪt】(刺激，使興奮)，所變化而來。

11. for one thing【θɪŋ】 ... ; for another【əˋnʌðɚ】 ...
    一來…，二來…

12. artist【ˋɑrtɪst】 名詞 藝術家，藝人

13. appear【əˋpɪr】 動詞 出現

14. so + 形容詞／副詞 + that 句　如此地…以致於

15. bear【bɛr】 動詞 忍受

16. boring【ˋborɪŋ】 形容詞 無聊的
    *由動詞 bore【bor】(使厭煩)，所變化而來。

17. without【wɪˋðaʊt】 介係詞 無，沒有

18. deciding【dɪ`saɪdɪŋ】 形容詞 決定性的

  *由動詞 decide【dɪ`saɪd】(決定),所變化而來。

19. in + V-ing = when + V-ing 在做⋯時

20. choose【tʃuz】 動詞 選擇

21. broken【`brokən】 形容詞 破碎的,損壞的

  *由動詞 break【brek】(打破),所變化而來。

練習題

I. 連貫式翻譯(一)

1. 我喜歡看落葉。

2. 正在飄落的葉子真的是很美的。

3. 有時候我會撿起落葉。

4. 落葉可以做書籤。

5. 書中的落葉給我清新的感受。

II. 連貫式翻譯(二)

1. 瑪莉喜歡看恐怖電影。

2. 她覺得恐怖電影很刺激。

3. 但是,有時候她看恐怖電影的時候會覺得害怕。

4. 即使如此,她還是不喜歡看文藝片。

5. 她覺得文藝片太無聊了。

III. 請找出《實際運用短文 - Kelly's Music Life》一文中有運用到本單元教學討論的「V-ing或p.p.做形容詞」

英文文法 不就 學會了　　187

之處，並將該部分劃上底線。

解答

Part 9

I. (註：畫線部分為「V-ing或p.p.做形容詞」之處)

1	I like to watch <u>falling</u> leaves.
2	<u>Falling</u> leaves are really beautiful.
3	Sometimes I pick up the <u>fallen</u> leaves.
4	<u>Fallen</u> leaves can be bookmarkers.
5	The <u>fallen</u> leaves in the book make me <u>refreshed</u>.

II.

1	Mary likes to watch horror movies.
2	She feels horror movies are very <u>exciting</u>.
3	However, sometimes she feels <u>scared</u> when she watches horror movies.
4	Even so, she still dislikes watching literary films.
5	She feels literary films are too <u>boring</u>.

III.

1. Sometime she feels really <u>exhausted</u>, but most of the time she feels her work is very <u>interesting</u> and <u>exciting</u>.

2. For another, she likes music so much that she can't bear a <u>boring</u> life without music.

3. For her, music is a <u>deciding</u> factor in choosing a job.

4. Without music, life may be <u>broken</u> for her.

現在進行式

重點一

在上一章，我們學習了動詞的「現在分詞」，而現在進行式的句型就需要用到現在分詞。

1. 現在進行式：主詞＋be動詞＋V-ing 【某人正在…】

例1：My children <u>are playing</u> in the park.

我們小孩正在公園玩。

例2：He <u>is eating</u> breakfast.

他正在吃早餐。

例3：My father <u>is singing</u> in the bathroom.

我爸爸正在浴室唱歌。

例4：I <u>am brushing</u> my teeth.

我正在刷牙。

2. 現在進行式的疑問句型：

(1) Be動詞＋主詞＋V-ing...? 【某人正在…?】

肯定簡答 Yes, 主詞＋be動詞.

　　　　是的，某人是。

肯定詳答 Yes, (主詞＋be動詞.) 主詞＋be動詞＋V-ing...

　　　　是的，(某人是。) 某人正在…

例1：Is it raining?

正在下雨嗎?

肯定簡答 Yes, it is. 是的。

肯定詳答1 Yes, it is raining. 是的，正在下雨。

肯定詳答2 Yes, it is. It is raining. 是的，正在下雨。

例2：Are they playing in the playground?

他們正在操場玩嗎？

肯定簡答 Yes, they are.

是的，他們是。

肯定詳答1 Yes, they are playing in the playground.

是的，他們正在操場玩。

肯定詳答2 Yes, they are. They are playing in the playground.

是的，他們是，他們正在操場玩。

(2) Be動詞＋主詞＋V-ing...?　【某人正在…?】

否定簡答 No, 主詞＋be動詞＋not(可用縮寫體).

不，某人不是。

否定詳答 No, (主詞＋be動詞＋not.) (可用縮寫體)

主詞＋be動詞＋not＋V-ing...

不，(某人不是。)某人沒有正在…

例1：Is John taking a bath?

約翰正在洗澡嗎？

否定簡答 No, he is not(或isn't).

不，他沒有。

否定詳答1 No, hc is not taking a bath.

不，他沒有正在洗澡。

否定詳答2 No, he is not(或isn't). He is not taking a bath.

不，他沒有，他沒有正在洗澡。

例2：Are your students reading English books?

你的學生正在讀英文書嗎？

否定簡答 No, they are not（或aren't）.

不，他們不是。

否定詳答1 No, they are not reading English books.

不，他們沒有正在讀英文書。

否定詳答2 No, they are not（或aren't）. They are not reading

English books.

不，他們沒有，他們沒有正在讀英文書。

重點二

疑問詞開頭的現在進行式句型

1.

問	What + be動詞 + 主詞 + V-ing...? 【某人正在…？】
答	主詞 + be動詞 + Ving... 【某人正在…】

例1：

問 What are you doing? 你正在做甚麼？

答 I am playing the guitar. 我正在彈吉他。

例2：

問 What is your mother doing? 你的母親正在做甚麼？

答 She is cooking dinner. 她正在煮晚餐。

例3：

問 What is Kevin reading? 凱文正在讀甚麼？

答 He is reading a magazine. 他正在讀雜誌。

例4：

問 What are the students studying? 這些學生正在讀甚麼？

答 They are studying math. 他們正在讀數學。

2.

問句	Who + is + V-ing...? 【誰正在…？】
簡答	主詞 + be動詞. 【是某人】
詳答	主詞 + be動詞 + V-ing... 【某人正在…】

例1： Who is singing?

誰在唱歌？

簡答 Vicky is.

是維琪。

詳答 Vicky is singing.

維琪正在唱歌

例2： Who is washing the clothes?

誰正在洗衣服？

簡答 My students are.

是我的學生們。

詳答 My students are washing the clothes.

我們學生們正在洗衣服。

英文文法 不小心就 學會了   193

例3：Who is talking on the phone?

誰正在講電話？

簡答 Jane is.

是珍。

詳答 Jane is talking on the phone.

珍正在講電話。

例4：Who is playing the piano?

誰正在彈鋼琴？

簡答 My younger sister is.

是我妹妹。

詳答 My younger sister is playing the piano.

我妹妹正在彈鋼琴。

重點三

Look! 或 Listen! 開頭

1. Look! + 現在進行式的句子

2. Listen! + 現在進行式的句子

例1：Look! They are playing basketball.

瞧！他們正在打籃球。

例2：Look! John is kissing his girlfriend.

瞧！約翰正在親吻他的女朋友。

例3：Listen! Someone is playing the violin.

聽！某人正在拉小提琴。

例4：Listen! The students are singing an English song.

聽！學生們正在唱英文歌。

重點四：無進行式的動詞

有些動詞不能用在現在進行式的句型裡，以下為常見的，無進行式的動詞：

1. 感官動詞

hear(聽到), see(看見), taste(品嚐), smell(聞起來), feel(感覺)

2. 心態動詞

agree(同意), believe(相信), forget(忘記), know(知道),

recognize(認可), remember(記得), understand(了解)

3. 情緒動詞

desire(渴望), forgive(原諒), hate(討厭), hope(希望),

like(喜歡), love(喜愛), prefer(偏好), want(想要)

4. 表位置的動詞

stand(坐落), sit(坐落), lie(位於)

5. 表擁有的動詞

belong(屬於), have(有), own(擁有)

例1：I am having a new car. (為錯誤的句子)

→I have a new car. (為正確的句子)

我有一台新車。

例2：He is loving Lisa. (為錯誤的句子)

→He loves Lisa. (為正確的句子)

他愛麗莎。

實際運用短文 Track 021

Sally and Kevin Are in a Park

Sally and Kevin are taking a walk in a park. They see many people along the way. Some are walking a dog. Others are jogging. And still others are playing with balls. Moreover, there are birds flying in the sky, and there are some ducks swimming on the lake, too. They really enjoy everything that they see in the park.

莎莉和凱文在公園裡

莎莉和凱文正在公園裡散步。沿路上他們看到很多人。有些人正在遛狗，有些人正在慢跑，還有些人正在打球。此外，天空中有鳥兒正在飛翔；湖面上也有鴨子正在游泳。他們真的很享受在公園裡所看見的每件事物。

1. talk a walk 　動詞片語　散步

2. along the way 　介係詞片語　沿路，一路上

3. some..., others..., and many/still others...
   有些…，有些…，還有些…

4. walk【wɔk】動詞　遛狗

5. jog【dʒɑg】動詞　慢跑

6. play【ple】動詞　打球

7. moreover【mor`ovɚ】副詞　此外

8. bird【bɝd】名詞　鳥

9. fly【flaɪ】動詞　飛

10. sky【skaɪ】名詞　天空

11. duck【dʌk】名詞　鴨子

12. swim【swɪm】動詞　游泳

13. lake【lek】名詞　湖

14. enjoy【ɪn`dʒɔɪ】動詞　喜愛，享受

練習題

I. 連貫式翻譯(一)

1. 操場有很多學生正在運動。

2. 有些學生在打籃球。

3. 有些學生在打棒球。

4. 還有些學生在慢跑。

5. 但有幾個學生只站著聊天。

II. 句子改寫(請將下列句子的時態改寫為「現在進行式」)

1. Vincent often writes poems at night.

2. They chat with each other on the phone every day.

3. I sometimes go shopping downtown.

4. He studies English every night.

5. Mr. and Mrs. Wang usually take a walk in a park.

III. 請找出《實際運用短文 - Sally and Kevin Are in a Park》
一文中有運用到本單元教學討論的「be + V-ing (現在
進行式)」之處,並將該部分劃上底線。

解答

I.

1	There are many students exercising on the playground.
2	Some are playing basketball.
3	Others are playing baseball.
4	And still others are jogging.
5	But some students are just standing and chatting.

II.

1	Vincent is writing poems (now).
2	They are chatting with each other on the phone (now).
3	I am going shopping downtown (now).
4	He is studying English (now).
5	Mr. and Mrs. Wang are taking a walk in a park (now).

III.

1. Sally and Kevin <u>are taking</u> a walk in a park.

2. Some <u>are walking</u> a dog.

3. Others <u>are jogging</u>.

4. And still others <u>are playing</u> with balls.

5. Moreover, there <u>are</u> birds <u>flying</u> in the sky, and there <u>are</u> some ducks <u>swimming</u> on the lake, too.

英文 ENGLISH

GRAMMAR 文法

不小心就 學會了

現在完成式

重點一

在第十章，我們學習了動詞的「過去分詞」，而現在完成式的句型就需要用到過去分詞。

*現在完成式肯定句：

主詞 + have / has + p.p.　【某人已經…】

*現在完成式否定句：

主詞 + have / has + not + p.p.　【某人尚未…】

*現在完成式疑問句：

Have/Has + 主詞 + p.p.…?　【某人已經…了嗎?】

重點二

使用時機：

1. 某一個動作從過去的某一個時間點開始，一直持續到現在的時間剛好完成。經常和already(已經), not...yet(尚未), just(剛剛)連用。

例1：The Wang family <u>have just left</u>.

王氏一家人剛離開。

例2：My boss is not here. He <u>has gone</u> to Chia-yi.

我老闆不在這裡。他已經去嘉義了。

例3：My daughter <u>has just finished</u> her homework.

我女兒剛完成她的家課。

例4：We <u>have not paid</u> the bill <u>yet</u>.

我們還沒有付帳單。

例5：<u>Have</u> you <u>already drunk</u> the tea?

你已經喝茶了嗎?

2. 指從過去到現在的經驗。經常和ever(曾經), never(從未), so far
   (迄今), once(一次), twice(兩次), many times(很多次)…連用。

例1：<u>Have</u> you <u>ever seen</u> my husband?
　　你曾經見過我先生嗎?

例2：I <u>have never been</u> to America.
　　我從未去過美國。

例3：Kelly <u>has been</u> to Hong Kong <u>many times</u>.
　　凱莉去過香港好多次。

例4：My brother <u>has visited</u> three countries <u>so far</u>.
　　我哥哥到目前為止已經去過三個國家。

3. 指某個動作從過去到現在，已經累積多少的時間。常和
   「for + 一段時間」或「since+過去時間/過去式句子」連用。
   *since【sɪns】 介係詞 或 副詞連接詞 自從…

例1：I <u>have lived</u> in Taipei <u>for three years</u>.
　　我住在台北三年了。

例2：Mark <u>has lived</u> in America <u>since 2010</u>.
　　從2010年起馬克就住在美國了。

例3：Bill <u>has worked</u> in Kaohsiung <u>since he got married</u>.
　　比爾自從結婚後就在高雄工作。

Living in Taipei

I have lived in Taipei for three years. And I have visited some famous places since my first year in Taipei. Among them, I like to visit National Chiang Kai-shek Memorial Hall the most. I have been there for more than 10 times. Most of the time I go there for a concert by the National Chinese Ochestra. And I have been to over six concerts there. However, there are still many places that I haven't visited yet. I have worked in a publishing company since I first came to Taipei. Since then, I have been very busy with my work. That's why I don't have much time to visit many places in Taipei. But I hope I can visit more places when I have free time.

住在台北

我已經住在台北三年了。而且從我第一年在台北起，我已經去過一些有名的地方。其中，我最喜歡去的地方就是中正紀念堂。我已經去過那裡超過十次了。大多數的時候我去那裡是為了台灣國樂團的音樂會。而我已經去那裡聽過六次以上的音樂會了。然而，仍然有很多地方我還沒去過。從我一開始來台北，就在一家出版公司工作。從那時起我就忙著工作。那就是為何我沒有很多時間去逛台北的很多地方。但是我希望我有空時可以去更多的地方。

重點註解 ━━━━━━➤

Track 022

1. live【lɪv】 動詞 生活

2. visit【`vɪzɪt】 動詞 參觀，拜訪

3. famous【`feməs】 形容詞 有名的

4. among【ə`mʌŋ】 介係詞 在…之中 (通常用在三者以上)

5. National Chiang Kai-shek Memorial Hall
   名詞片語 中正紀念堂

6. more than 介係詞片語 超過 (= over)

7. concert【`kɑnsət】 名詞 音樂會

8. National Chinese Ochestra 名詞片語 台灣國樂團

9. not…yet 表「尚未…」

10. publishing【`pʌblɪʃɪŋ】 形容詞 出版的

11. more【mor】 形容詞比較級 更多的 (many/more/most)

練習題

I. 連貫式翻譯 (一)

1. 我學古箏已經二十幾年了。

2. 我也已經從藝術學校畢業了。

3. 從事古箏教學已經三個月。

4. 自從畢業起，我舉行超過五次以上的古箏音樂會。

5. 而且已經和許多學生和古箏演奏家成為朋友。

英文文法 不小心就學會了　　205

II. 連貫式翻譯 (二)

1. 老師問我:「你學英文多久了呢?」
2. 我回答:「我學英文已經一年了。」
3. 老師接著說:「我原本以為你已經學英文超過三年了。」
4. 然後我問她:「為什麼你會以為我已經學英文那麼久了?」
5. 她回答說:「因為你已經閱讀很多篇超過一千個基本單字的文章了。」

III. 請找出《實際運用短文 - Living in Taipei》一文中有運用到本單元教學討論的「have/has + p.p. (現在完成式)」之處,並將該部分劃上底線。

解答

I.

1	I have studied zither for more than twenty years.
2	I have also graduated from the art school.
3	I have taught zither for three months.
4	Since graduation, I have held zither concerts over five times.
5	And I have made friends with many students and zither musicians.

II.

1	The teacher asked me, "How long have you studied English?"
2	I answered, "I have studied English for one year."
3	The teacher then said, "I initially think you have studied English for more than three years."
4	Then I asked her, "Why do you think I have studied English for so long?"
5	She answered, "Because you have read many articles with more than 1000 basic words."

III.

1. I <u>have lived</u> in Taipei for three years.

2. And I <u>have visited</u> some famous places since my first year in Taipei.

3. I <u>have been</u> there for more than 10 times.

4. And I <u>have been</u> to over six concerts there.

5. However, there are still many places that I <u>haven't visited</u> yet.

6. I <u>have worked</u> in a publishing company since I first came to Taipei.

7. Since then, I <u>have been</u> very busy with my work.

英文 ENGLISH

GRAMMAR 文法

不小心就 學會了

過去進行式

重點一

在第十章，我們學習了動詞的「現在分詞」，而過去進行式的句型就需要用到現在分詞。

過去進行式：主詞 + 過去式be動詞(was/were) + V-ing

重點二

表示「過去某個時間點」正在進行的動作，要有表示過去時間點的時間片語。

例1：He <u>was playing</u> the guitar <u>at nine o'clock last night</u>.
　　　他昨晚九點時在彈吉他。

例2：They <u>were studying</u> English <u>at ten o'clock this</u>
　　　<u>morning</u>.
　　　他們今天早上十點在讀英文。

重點三

在過去，若有兩個動作一短一長，短的動作發生在長的動作之內，長者用過去進行式，短者用過去簡單式。

例1：He <u>saw</u> her while he <u>was crossing</u> the road.
　　　他在過馬路時看見了她。

　　　解析：過馬路為長動作，所以用進行式(was crossing)。「看見」為發生在「過馬路時」的短動作，所以用簡單式(saw)。

　　　＊while【hwaɪl】(副詞連接詞)正當…

例2：When Jane <u>came</u> to see his father, he <u>was eating</u> his lunch.

當珍來見他的父親時，他正在吃午餐。

解析：吃午餐為長動作，所以用進行式(was eating)。

「來」為發生在「吃午餐」時的短動作，所以用簡單式(came)。

重點四

表示過去同時進行的「兩個長動作」，兩個動作都用過去進行式。

例1：While I <u>was preparing</u> lunch, they <u>were watching</u> TV.

當我正在準備午餐時，他們正看著電視。

例2：While Mary <u>was</u> writing a letter, John <u>was reading</u> a novel.

當瑪莉在寫信時，約翰在讀小説。

A Family Fight

My family and I had a fight last night. Last night, while Mother was preparing dinner, my two younger sisters and I were watching TV in the living room. Then we were having dinner together when my friend Lisa called me. Lisa wanted me to come to her house soon to help her with the homework. So I went to her house at once without finishing my dinner and washing the dishes. When I came back home, both my sisters blamed me and then we had a fight when someone was knocking at the door. I opened the door and found it was Lisa. Thanks to Lisa's explanation, we finally ended the fight.

家庭爭吵

我的家人跟我昨晚發生爭吵。昨晚，正當媽媽準備晚餐時，我的兩個妹妹跟我在客廳裡看電視。然後正當我們一起用晚餐時，我的朋友麗莎打電話給我。麗莎要我快點去她家幫她做家課。因此我馬上去她家而沒有吃完晚餐跟洗碗盤。當我回家時，我兩個妹妹都責備我，當我們隨後發生爭吵時有人在敲門。我打開門發現是麗莎。多虧了麗莎的解釋，我們終於停止了爭吵。

1. fight【faɪt】 名詞 爭吵

2. prepare【prɪ`pɛr】 動詞 準備

3. call【kɔl】 動詞 打電話

4. want + 人 + to + 原形動詞　要…人去…

5. soon【sun】 副詞 很快地

6. help + 人 + with + 名詞　幫助…人…

7. at once【æt】【wʌns】 介係詞片語 立刻，馬上

8. without + 名詞／V-ing　沒有…

9. finish【`fɪnɪʃ】+ 名詞／V-ing　完成…

10. wash【wɑʃ】 動詞 洗

11. dish【dɪʃ】 名詞 餐具，碗盤

12. blame【blem】 動詞 責備

13. knock【nɑk】 動詞 敲，擊

14. find【faɪnd】 動詞 發現(三態：find/found/found)

15. thanks to + 名詞／V-ing　多虧…

16. explanation【ˌɛksplə`neʃən】 名詞 解釋

17. finally【`faɪn!ɪ】 副詞 最後，終於

18. end【ɛnd】 動詞 結束，終止

練習題

I. 連貫式翻譯（一）

1. 我昨晚八點時在彈吉他。

2. 那時候我哥在客廳聽音樂，我媽在洗衣服。

3. 然後到了九點時，有人在敲門。

4. 我打開門，發現地上有一個蛋糕和一張卡片。

5. 正當我打開卡片時，大衛來電。。

6. 大衛和我哥已經是超過十年的好朋友了。

7. 大衛在電話中告訴我：「這是慶祝你哥哥今天早上贏得
   比賽的蛋糕。」

8. 當我把蛋糕拿進客廳時，媽媽正在看電視。

9. 而哥哥那時候正在洗澡。

10. 於是我跟媽媽把蛋糕吃了，只留下卡片給哥哥。

II. 請找出《實際運用短文 - A Family Fight》一文中有
運用到本單元教學討論的「was/were + V-ing（過去
進行式）」之處，並將該部分劃上底線。

解答

I.

1	I was playing the guitar at eight o'clock last night.
2	At that time, my older brother was listening to music in the living room, and my mother was washing the clothes.
3	Then at nine o'clock, someone was knocking at the door.
4	I opened the door and found there were a cake and a card on the ground.
5	When I was opening the card, David called me.
6	David and my older brother have been good friends for more than 10 years.
7	David told me on the phone, "This cake is for celebrating the game that your older brother won this morning."
8	When I took the cake to the living room, Mother was watching TV.
9	And my older brother was taking a bath then.
10	So Mother and I finished off the cake, and only left the card for my older brother.

Part
16

II.

1. Last night, while Mother <u>was preparing</u> dinner, my two younger sisters and I <u>were watching</u> TV in the living room.

2. Then we <u>were having</u> dinner together when my friend Lisa called me.

3. When I came back home, both my sisters blamed me and then we had a fight when someone <u>was knocking</u> at the door.

PART
17

過去完成式

重點一

在第十章,我們學習了動詞的「過去分詞」,而過去完成式的句型就需要用到過去分詞。

*過去完成式:主詞＋had＋p.p. 【某人已經…】

重點二

在過去,有兩個動作,一個先發生,一個後發生,先發生的用「過去完成式(had＋p.p.)」,後發生的用「過去簡單式(V-ed)」。

例1: The train <u>had left</u> when we <u>reached</u> the station.

我們抵達車站時火車已經開走了。

*解析:火車先走後,人才到。所以火車開走用過去完成式(had left),人到用過去簡單式(reached)

例2: When they <u>arrived</u>, July <u>had gone</u> home.

當他們抵達時,茱蒂已經回家了。

*解析:July先回家後,他們人才到。所以July回家用過去完成式(had gone),他們人到用過去簡單式(arrived)

例3: We <u>didn't want</u> to go. We <u>had been</u> to the temple the weekend before.

我們不想去。我們這個周末前就去過那個廟寺了。

*解析:先去過廟寺,所以用過去完成式(had been)。之後不想再去,所以用過去簡單式(didn't want)。

重點三

在過去某一特定時間點以前已完成的動作，常用「介係詞 by (在…之前) + 特定時間」或是「by the time (到了…的時候) + 句子」。

1. 句(過去完成式) + by + 特定時間.

例1：He <u>had finished</u> his homework <u>by yesterday morning</u>.
   昨天早上前他就完成了家課。

例2：They <u>had left</u> for Tainan <u>by 10 o'clock this morning</u>.
   今天早上十點前他們就動身前往台南了。

2. 句(過去完成式) + by the time + 句(過去式).

例1：My boss <u>had left</u> the office <u>by the time you called to me</u>.
   你打電話給我時，我們老闆已經離開辦公室了。

例2：The bus <u>had left</u> <u>by the time we reached the bus stop</u>.
   我們到公車站的時候，公車已經開走了。

It's Not My Day

I had an important meeting at 2 o'clock yesterday afternoon. I had to take a train to attend the meeting. Unluckily, I slept late the day before yesterday, so I got up very late yesterday. When I reached the train station, the train had already left. I had no choice but to take the next train. By the time I got to the meeting room, it was already 3:45 p.m., and the managers that I had to meet had left for their companies. They had finished the meeting by 3:30 p.m.. My boss blamed me badly for my neglect of duty. It was really not my day!

倒楣的一天

昨天下午兩點我有一個重要的會議。我必須搭火車去參加那個會議。不幸的是，前天我晚睡，所以昨天起得很晚。當我抵達火車站時，火車已經開走了。不得已我只好搭下一班火車。當我到達會議室時，已經是下午三點四十五分了，我必須碰面的經理們都已經離開回他們的公司。他們在三點半前已經開完會。我的老闆嚴厲地責備我怠忽職守。真是倒楣的一天!

1. important【ɪm`pɔrtnt】 形容詞 重要的

2. meetimg【`mitɪŋ】 名詞 會議

3. had to + V 過去式 必須

4. attend【ə`tɛnd】 動詞 出席，參加

5. unluckily【ʌn`lʌkɪlɪ】 副詞 不幸地

6. sleep【slip】 動詞 睡覺 (三態：sleep/slept/slept)

7. the day before yesterday 時間片語 前天

8. get up 動詞片語 起床 (三態：get/got/got 或 gotten)

9. reach【ritʃ】 動詞 抵達

10. train station【tren】【`steʃən】 名詞片語 火車站

11. already【ɔl`rɛdɪ】 副詞 已經

12. leave【liv】 動詞 離開 (三態：leave/left/left)

13. have no choice but to + V 不得不…

    choice【tʃɔɪs】 名詞 選擇

14. next【`nɛkst】 形容詞 下一班的，下一個的

15. get to + 地方 抵達…地方 (= reach + 地方 = arrive in/at + 地方)

16. manager【`mænɪdʒɚ】 名詞 經理

17. leave for + 地方 前往…地方

18. blame + 人 + for + 名詞／V-ing 因為…而責備…人

19. neglect【nɪg`lɛkt】 名詞 疏忽

20. duty【`djutɪ】 名詞 職責

21. not one's day 運氣不好的一天

英文文法 秒殺 學會了 221

練習題

I. 連貫式翻譯

1. 昨晚我到社區大學去上英文課。

2. 當我到教室時，老師和同學已經離開教室了。

3. 我打電話問我同學約翰為何教室空無一人。

4. 他告訴我說老師和同學七點十分前就離開前往運動公園 參加活動了。

5. 於是我立刻到運動公園去，但是當我抵達時，活動卻已 經結束了。

II. 選擇題

1. By the time Vicky got to the restaurant, they _____ their dinner.

(A)had finished (B) finished (C) finishing (D) have finished

2. He had left for the company when we _____ to his home.

(A)had come (B) come (C) came (D) coming

3. The boy had finished his homework before he _____ to school.

(A)goes (B) was going (C) went (D) gone

4. Mary _____ asleep in the classroom by 8:30 this morning.

(A)falls (B) fell (C) had fallen (D) was falling

5. When the police got to the bank, the robbers _____ away.

(A)run (B) ran (C) had run (D) running

III. 請找出《實際運用短文 - It's Not My Day》一文中有
運用到本單元教學討論的「had + p.p.(過去完成式)」
之處，並將該部分劃上底線。

解答

I.

1	I went to the community university to take the English class last night.
2	When I got to the classroom, the teacher and the students had already left.
3	I called my classmate John and asked him why the classroom was empty.
4	He told me that the teacher and the students had left for the sports park to join in an activity by 7:10 p.m..
5	So I immediately went to the sports park. But when I got there, the activity had already been over.

II.

1	A	2	C	3	C	4	C	5	C

III.

1. When I reached the train station, the train <u>had</u> already <u>left</u>.

2. By the time I got to the meeting room, it was already 3:45 p.m., and the managers that I had to meet <u>had left</u> for their companies.

3. They <u>had finished</u> the meeting by 3:30 p.m..

PART
18

未來式

重點一

未來式表達尚未發生的事情，常和表未來的時間副詞連用：

this afternoon(今天下午), tonight(今天晚上), tomorrow(明天),
tomorrow morning/afternoon/evening(明天早上/明天下午/明天
晚上), next 禮拜幾/week/month/季節/year(下個禮拜幾/下星期
/下個月/明年的…季節/明年)」, the day after tomorrow(後天),
in + 一段時間(再過…)

1. 未來式肯定句型：主詞 + will + 原形動詞

例1：He <u>will fly</u> to Hong Kong <u>tomorrow afternoon</u>.
　　 明天下午他要飛去香港。

例2：We <u>will go</u> to the movies <u>next week</u>.
　　 下周我們會去看電影。

例3：My family <u>will go</u> on a picnic <u>next Sunday</u>.
　　 下周日我們家要去野餐。

例4：The manager <u>will have</u> a meeting with us <u>in a few days</u>.
　　 過幾天這位經理將和我們一起開會。

2. 未來式否定句型：主詞 + will not + 原形動詞

　　*will not可縮寫為won't

例1：My boyfriend <u>will not wash</u> the dishes after meal.
　　 我男朋友用餐後不會洗碗。

例2：They <u>won't go</u> to the concert the day after tomorrow.
　　 他們後天不會去音樂會。

3. 未來式疑問句型：Will + 主詞 + 原形動詞...?

肯定簡答 Yes, 主詞 + will.

肯定詳答 Yes, (主詞 + will.) 主詞 + will + 原形動詞...

否定簡答 No, 主詞 + will not (或won't).

否定詳答 No,〔主詞 + will not (或won't).〕主詞 + will not
(或won't) + 原形動詞...

例1：<u>Will you play</u> basketball with me after school?
　　　放學後你會跟我一起打籃球嗎？

肯定簡答 Yes, I will.
　　　　是的，我會。

肯定詳答1 Yes, I will play basketball with you after school.
　　　　是，放學後我會跟你一起打籃球。

肯定詳答2 Yes, I will. I will play basketball with you after
school.
　　　　是的，我會。放學後我會跟你一起打籃球。

否定簡答 No, I will not. (或No, I won't).
　　　　不，我不會。

否定詳答1 No, I will not play basketball with you after school.
(或No, I won't play basketball with you after school.)
　　　　不，放學後我不會跟你一起打籃球。

否定詳答2 No, I will not. I will not play basketball with you
after school. (或No, I won't. I won't play basketball
with you after school.)
　　　　不，我不會。放學後我不會跟你一起打籃球。

例2：Will your mother cook dinner tonight?

今天晚上你的媽媽會煮晚餐嗎？

肯定簡答 Yes, she will.

是的，她會。

肯定詳答1 Yes, she will cook dinner tonight.

是的，今天晚上她會煮晚餐。

肯定詳答2 Yes, she will. She will cook dinner tonight.

是的，她會。今天晚上她會煮晚餐。

否定簡答 No, she will not.（或No, she won't）.

不，她不會。

否定詳答1 No, she will not cook dinner tonight.（或No, she won't cook dinner tonight.）

不，今天晚上她不會煮晚餐。

否定詳答2 No, she will not. She will not cook dinner tonight.（或No, she won't. She won't cook dinner tonight.）

不，她不會。今天晚上她不會煮晚餐。

重點二：will 和 be going to

will和be going to很多時候可通用，但仍有不同之處，如下：

1. be going to有事先計劃的意思，will並沒有經過事先的計劃。

例1：He has sold his car because he's going to work in Taipei.

他已經把車子賣了，因為他打算去台北工作。(有事先計劃)

例2：My son will be fifteen years old next year.

我兒子明年將十五歲.(沒有事先的計劃)

2. will表「長期或短期」的未來，be going to表「即刻的」未來。

例1：My husband <u>will come</u> back in three years.

三年後我先生會回來。

例2：We <u>are going to play</u> basketball after school.

放學後我們將打籃球。

重點三

「來去動詞」可用「現在進行式」代替「即將發生的未來式」：

常見的來去動詞：

come(來), go(去), leave(離開), start(出發), arrive(抵達),

return(返回), depart(離開), reach(到達)

例1：I <u>am leaving</u> for London.

我即將前往倫敦。

例2：The bus <u>is reaching</u> Ilan.

公車即將抵達宜蘭。

重點四

疑問詞開頭的未來式問句

1.

問	疑問詞 + will + 主詞 + 原形動詞...?
答	主詞 + will + 原形動詞...

例1：

問 When will you go to the library?

你何時要去圖書館？

答 I will go to the library tomorrow.

我明天要去圖書館。

例2：

問 When will they hold a party?

他們何時要舉行派對？

答 They will hold a party next Saturday.

他們下周六要舉行派對。

2.

問	疑問詞 + be動詞 + 主詞 + going to + 原形動詞...?
答	主詞 + be動詞 + going to + 原形動詞...

例1：

問 What are you going to do tonight?

你今晚要做什麼？

答 I am going to practice the guitar.

我今晚要練習吉他。

例2：

問 When is your wife going to school?

你的太太何時要去學校？

答 She is going to school at 5:00 this afternoon.

她今天下午五點要去學校。

My Dream

I will graduate from the university next month. And I will be 19 years old then. I have bought many books on job interviews because I am going to work in Taipei. I will leave for Taipei to find a job at the end of next month. Many of my friends wonder what I am going to do after graduation, and I tell them that my dream is to teach in a community university. Since I major in English and have great interest in music, I plan to teach English conversations and English songs and I will also sing every song that I teach my students together with them. I think teaching in a community university is the best way to combine my specialty with interest. I really hope I will make my dream come true.

我的夢想

我下個月將從大學畢業。而那時候我將十九歲。我已經買了很多有關工作面試的書，因為我即將去台北工作。下個月底我將前往台北找工作。我的很多朋友對於我畢業後要做什麼感到好奇，我告訴他們我的夢想是在社區大學教書。既然我主修英文，而且對音樂有濃厚的興趣，我打算教英文會話及英文歌曲，而且我會跟我的學生一同歡唱每首教給他們的歌曲。我覺得在社大教書是結合我的專業跟興趣最好的方法。我真的希望我會使我的夢想成真。

Track 025

1. graduate【`grædʒʊ,et】 動詞 畢業

2. university【,junə`vɝ·sətɪ】 名詞 大學

3. then【ðɛn】 副詞 那時候 (= at that time)

4. buy【baɪ】 動詞 買 (三態:buy/bought/bought)

5. on【ɑn】 介係詞 有關

6. interview【`ɪntə,vju】 名詞 面試

7. leave for 動詞片語 前往

8. find【faɪnd】 動詞 找,發現

9. at the end of 介係詞片語 在⋯末端,在⋯結尾

10. wonder【`wʌndə·】 動詞 好奇,想知道

11. community university【kə`mjunətɪ】【,junə`vɝ·sətɪ】
    名詞片語 社區大學

12. since【sɪns】 副詞連接詞 既然,因為

13. major in 動詞片語 主修

14. interest【`ɪntərɪst】 名詞 興趣

15. plan to + V 計畫,打算要⋯

16. conversation【,kɑnvə·`seʃən】 名詞 會話

17. way + to V 做⋯的方式

18. combine + A + with + B 結合A跟B

19. come true 動詞片語 成真

I. 連貫式翻譯 (一)

1. 籃球賽今天何時開始?

2. 將在下午三點開始。

3. 你何時要去體育館呢?

4. 我快要出門吃午餐了。

5. 吃完午餐後,我將直接去體育館看球賽。

II. 連貫式翻譯 (二)

1. 你們何時將要結婚?

2. 我們將在明年舉辦婚禮。

3. 婚後我們會在美國度蜜月。

4. 婚後我們不會搬出去。

5. 我們會繼續跟父母親同住。

III. 將下列句子加入will改寫為未來式。

1. I go to the movies. (tomorrow)

2. Kelly goes to church. (next week)

3. There is a baseball game at the stadium. (tonight)

4. My parents go to the sports park. (after work)

5. The president comes here. (the day after tomorrow)

解答

I.

1	When will the basketball game start today?
2	It will start at 3 o'clock this afternoon.
3	When will you go to the gym?
4	I am going out for lunch.
5	After lunch, I will directly go the the gym to watch the game.

II.

1	When will you get married?
2	We will hold our wedding ceremony next year.
3	After getting married, we will have our honeymoon in America.
4	After marriage, we will not (或won't) move out.
5	We will continue to live with our parents.

III.

1	I will go to the movies tomorrow.
2	Kelly will go to church next week.
3	There will be a baseball game at the stadium tonight.
4	My parents will go to the sports park after work.
5	The president will come here the day after tomorrow.

IV.

1. I will graduate from the university next month.

2. And I will be 19 years old then.

3. I have bought many books on job interviews because I am going to work in Taipei.

4. I will leave for Taipei to find a job at the end of next month.

5. Many of my friends wonder what I am going to do after graduation, and I tell them that my dream is to teach in a community university.

6. Since I major in English and have great interest in music, I plan to teach English conversations and English songs and I will also sing every song that I teach my students together with them.

7. I really hope I will make my dream come true.

英文 ENGLISH
GRAMMAR 文法
不小心就 學會了

PART
19

被動式

被動式解析：

在第十章，我們學習了動詞的「過去分詞」，而被動式的句型就需要用到過去分詞。

重點一

簡單式被動

1.

現在簡單式被動

主詞 + be動詞(am/is/are) + p.p. + (by + 受詞)

例1：The door is opened by Sally.

門被莎莉打開。

例2：The book is written by Vicky.

這書是維琪所寫的。

2.

過去簡單式被動

主詞 + was/were + p.p. + (by + 受詞)

例1：The building was built by us in 2013.

這棟大樓是我們在2013年所建造的。

例2：The cars were washed by my father.

這些車是我爸爸所清洗的。

重點二

進行式被動：進行式與被動式的結合

1.

現在進行式被動

主詞 + be動詞(am/is/are) + being + p.p. + (by + 受詞)

例1：At present a new park <u>is being built</u> in this community.

目前一座新公園正在這個社區建蓋中。

例2：The sick child <u>is being checked</u> by a doctor.

這個生病的小孩正由醫生檢查中。

2.

過去進行式被動

主詞 + was/were + being + p.p. + (by + 受詞)

例1：I <u>was being blamed by</u> my mother when you called

me last night.

你昨晚打電話給我的時候，我正被我的媽媽責罵中。

例2：The window <u>was being opened by</u> a thief when we got

home this afternoon.

今天下午我們到家時，窗戶正被一個小偷打開中。

重點三

未來簡單式被動：未來式與被動式的結合

*主詞 + will + be + p.p. + (by + 受詞)

例1：Your class <u>will be taught by</u> Miss Ho next spring.

　　　明年春天你們班將由何老師所教導。

例2：The gift <u>will be bought by</u> her boyfriend tomorrow.

　　　禮物明天將由她的男朋友所購買。

重點四

完成式被動：完成式與被動式的結合

1.

現在完成式被動

主詞 + have/has + been + p.p. + (by + 受詞)

例1：The gas <u>has been checked by</u> your father.

　　　瓦斯已經被你的父親檢查過了。

例2：The rooms <u>have been cleaned by</u> me.

　　　這些房間已經被我打掃過了。

2.

過去完成式被動

主詞 + had + been + p.p. + (by + 受詞)

例1：The letter <u>had been delivered by</u> the postman when I reached the post office.

當我到達郵局的時候，信已經被郵差送走了。

例2：The cake <u>had been eaten by</u> the students when the teacher came to the classroom.

當老師來到教室時，蛋糕已經被學生們吃掉了。

重點五

有助動詞 (should/can/must/may) 的被動式

✽主詞 + 助動詞 + be + p.p. + (by + 受詞)

例1：More training <u>should be offered by</u> my company.

更多訓練應由我們公司所提供。

例2：The window <u>may be broken by</u> a thief.

這個窗戶也許是被小偷所打破的。

例3：The work <u>can be finished by</u> Mr. Chen.

這工作可由陳先生完成。

例4：The floor <u>must be cleaned by</u> Mary.

地板一定是瑪莉所打掃的。

重點六

無被動語態的動詞：英文有些動詞無被動語態，常見的如下：

1. 感覺類動詞：

look(看起來)/sound(聽起來)/smell(聞起來)/taste(嚐起來)/
feel(感覺起來)/seem(似乎)

例1：The cake tastes good. (為正確的句子)

　　→The cake is tasted good. (為不正確的句子)

　　這蛋糕好吃。

例2：This idea sounds good. (為正確的句子)

　　→This idea is sounded good. (為不正確的句子)

　　這主意聽起來不錯。

2. 事實類動詞：

happen(發生)/occur(發生)/take place(舉行)/break out(爆發)/
belong to(屬於)/exist(存在)/consist of(包含)/arrive(抵達)

例1：The game will take place next Friday. (正確)

　　→The game will be taken place next Friday. (不正確)

　　比賽將在下周五舉行。

例2：The watch belongs to me. (為正確的句子)

　　→The watch is belonged to me. (為不正確的句子)

　　這隻錶是我的。

Score

I am often blamed for low score on tests. I try to study hard, but may be disturbed by many things. My classmates often ask me to play basketball with them. And my good friends usually invite me to join in their activities. I know I will be punished by some of my strict teachers if I don't get a good grade, but I just can't resist the temptation to be with my classmates and friends and have a good time with them. Although I have been blamed or punished for low socres many times, I still cherish friendship more than my score.

分數

我常常因為考試低分而被責罵。我嘗試用功，但也許會被很多事情干擾。我的同學常常要我跟他們一起打籃球。而且我的好朋友經常邀請我加入他們的活動。我知道如果我沒有拿好成績，我會被一些嚴格的老師所處罰，但我就是無法抵抗想跟同學及朋友在一起度過美好時光的誘惑。雖然我已經因為低分被責備及處罰很多次了，我還是珍惜友誼多於分數。

1. blame【blem】 動詞 責備

2. low【lo】 形容詞 低的

3. score【skor】 名詞 分數，成績

4. test【tɛst】 名詞 測驗，考試

5. try + to V 嘗試去做…

6. disturb【dɪs`tɝb】 動詞 妨礙，打擾

7. ask + 人 + to + V 要某人去…

8. invite + 人 + to + V 邀請某人去…

9. join in 動詞片語 加入 (= take part in = participate in)

10. activity【æk`tɪvətɪ】 名詞 活動

11. punish【`pʌnɪʃ】 動詞 處罰

12. strict【strɪkt】 形容詞 嚴格的

13. grade【gred】 名詞 成績，分數

14. resist【rɪ`zɪst】 動詞 抵抗

15. temptation【tɛmp`teʃən】 名詞 誘惑

16. although【ɔl`ðo】 副詞連接詞 雖然

    Although (= Though) + 句, 句.

17. cherish【`tʃɛrɪʃ】 動詞 珍惜

18. friendship【`frɛndʃɪp】 名詞 友誼

19. more為much的副詞比較級，表「更多」，修飾cherish

I. 連貫式翻譯

1. 我昨天過馬路時被機車撞了。

2. 接著我馬上被送去鄰近的醫院。

3. 在我到達醫院之前，撞我的騎士已經先到了醫院。

4. 他跟我道歉，還說已經受到我家人的責備。

5. 還說新的衣物已經放在我病房的床上了，也會替我付醫藥費。

II. 將下列句子改寫為被動式。

1. I have finished the homework.

2. My mother grows these flowers.

3. She will clean the room.

4. Mr. Chen invited her to dinner.

5. The construction workers are building the bridge.

III. 請找出《實際運用短文 - Score》一文中有運用到本單元
　　教學討論的各種時態的「被動式」之處，並將該部分劃
　　上底線。

解答

I.

1	I was hit by a motorcycle when I was crossing the road.
2	Then I was immediately taken to a nearby hospital.

英文文法 秘密 學會了　　　245

3	Before I got to the hospital, the motorcyclist that hit me had reached there.
4	He apologized to me and said that he had been blamed by my family.
5	He also said that new clothes had been put on the bed in my ward, and he would pay the medical fee for me.

II.

1	The homework has been finished by me.
2	These flowers are grown by my mother.
3	The room will be cleaned by her.
4	She was invited to dinner by Mr. Chen.
5	The bridge is being built by the construction workers.

III.

1. I am often blamed for low score on tests.

2. I try to study hard, but may be disturbed by many things.

3. I know I will be punished by some of my strict teachers if I don't get a good grade, but I just can't resist the temptation to be with my classmates and friends and have a good time with them.

4. Although I have been blamed or punished for low socres many times, I still cherish friendship more than my score.

對等連接詞

對等連接詞

顧名思義，主要功用就是連接兩個「詞性及結構對等」的單字、片語，或句子。

重點一

主要有四個：
and(而且，和)；or(或)；but(但是)；so(因此，所以)

重點二

主要位置：單字/片語/句子(,) + 對等連接詞(and/or/but/so) + 單字/片語/句子.

例1：Vicky and Kelly <u>sang</u> and <u>danced</u> all night.
維琪和凱莉通宵唱歌跳舞。

*解析：and連接兩個過去式動詞：sang和danced

例2：Do you want <u>coffee</u> or <u>tea</u>?
你想要咖啡還是茶?

*解析：or連接兩個名詞：coffee和tea

例3：<u>It is hot in summer in Kaohsiung</u>, but <u>it is not very cold in winter</u>.

高雄夏天熱，但冬天不會很冷。

*解析：but連接兩個現在式的句子：it is hot in summer in Kaohsiung和it is not very cold in winter

例4：<u>He was sick</u>, so <u>he didn't go to school yesterday</u>.

他生病，所以昨天沒有上學。

*解析：so連接兩個過去式的句子：he was sick和he
didn't go to school yesterday

重點三

對等連接詞也可以「放在句首」，承接上句的意思「引導另一
句」做說明之用。

＊<u>對等連接詞(And/Or/But/So) ＋ 單句</u>.

例1：John doesn't like English, and Mary doesn't like it,
either. <u>But</u> I like it very much.

約翰不喜歡英文，而且瑪莉也不喜歡英文。但是我很
喜歡英文。

*解析：But放句首，和前句的意思形成對比。

例2：Dr. Huang asks Helen to go to bed early and eat more
vegetables. <u>So</u> she can improve her skin.

黃醫師要海倫早點睡覺及多吃蔬菜。如此她可以改善皮膚。

*解析：So放句首，延續前句的意思作因果關係的說明。

Track 027

Xinzhuang Sports Park

I have lived in Xinzhuang for three years. I like Xinzhuang a lot because life is convenient here. Besides, there are many attractions in Xinzhuang, such as Xingzhuang Temple Street, Xingzhuang Culture & Arts Center, and Xinzhuang Sports Park. Among these attractions, I like Xinzhuang Sports Park most because it is very beautiful, and you can do many things there. When I have free time, I often go there to take a walk or go jogging. And if you like to watch sports games, you can watch professional baseball games in Xinzhuang Baseball Stadium, and basketball games in Xinzhuang Gymnasium in Xinzhuang Sports Park. Many people also dance, play balls, or walk a dog there. It is really a good place to exercise, relax and have lots of fun!

新莊運動公園

我住在新莊已經三年了。我很喜歡新莊因為這裡的生活很便利。此外，新莊有很多景點，比如說新莊廟街、新莊文化藝術中心，以及新莊運動公園。在這些景點之中，我最喜歡新莊運動公園，因為它很美麗，而且你可以在那裡做很多事情。當我有空的時候，我常常去那裡散步或慢跑。

而如果你喜歡看運動比賽的話，你可以在新莊運動公園裡面的新莊棒球場看職業棒球賽，在新莊體育館裡面看籃球賽。許多人也在那裡跳舞、打球，或是遛狗。它真的是一個運動、放鬆，以及擁有很多樂趣的好去處！

重點註解 ➞ Track 027

1. Xinzhuang Sports Park （名詞片語）新莊運動公園
   sports【sports】（形容詞）運動的
2. convenient【kən`vinjənt】（形容詞）便利的
3. besides【br`saɪdz】（副詞）此外
   = also = in addition = moreover = furthermore
4. attraction【ə`trækʃən】（名詞）吸引力，景點
5. Xingzhuang Temple Street （名詞片語）新莊廟街
   temple【`tɛmp!】（名詞）寺廟
   street【strit】（名詞）街道
6. Xingzhuang Culture & Arts Center （名詞片語）新莊文化藝術中心
   culture【`kʌltʃɚ】（名詞）文化
   art【ɑrt】（名詞）藝術
   center【`sɛntɚ】（名詞）中心
7. most （副詞最高級）最（副詞三級：much/more/most）
8. take a walk （動詞片語）散步
9. go + V-ing (jogging) 從事…
   jog【dʒɑg】（動詞）慢跑

10. watch【wɑtʃ】 動詞 觀看

11. professional【prə`fɛʃən!】 形容詞 專業的，職業性的

12. baseball【`bes,bɔl】 名詞 棒球

13. stadium【`stedɪəm】 名詞 體育場，球場

14. basketball【`bæskɪt,bɔl】 名詞 籃球

15. gymnasium【dʒɪm`nezɪəm】 名詞 體育館

16. dance【dæns】 動詞 跳舞

17. walk【wɔk】 動詞 遛狗

18. exercise【`ɛksə,saɪz】 動詞 運動

19. relax【rɪ`læks】 動詞 放鬆

20. lots of＋不可數名詞＝a lot of＋不可數名詞
    ＝much＋不可數名詞　很多…

21. fun【fʌn】 名詞 樂趣

練習題

I. 連貫式翻譯

1. 我和我弟有很多相似及相異點。

2. 以相似點來說，我們都喜歡自由，以及願意接受新事物。

3. 我們都喜歡運動，以及品嚐美食。

4. 以相異點來說，我很喜歡唱歌，我弟則不。

5. 我很喜歡喝茶，我弟卻比較喜歡喝果汁。

II. 將下列句子用對等連接詞連接成一句。

1. He grows flowers in the garden. He grows vegetables in the garden.

2. She likes to watch basketball games. She doesn't like to watch baseball games.

3. You can play the guitar. You can also play the piano.

4. Tom was sick yesterday. Tom didn't go to school yesterday.

5. I will clean my room tonight. I will do my homework tonight. I will not go out with you.

III. 請找出《實際運用短文 - Xinzhuang Sports Park》一文中有運用到本單元教學討論的「對等連接詞」之處，並將該部分劃上底線。

解答

I.

1	There are many similarities and differences between my younger brother and me.
2	As for similarities, we both like freedom, and are willing to accept new things.
3	We both like to exercise, and try delicious foods.
4	As to differences, I like to sing very much, but my younger brother doesn't.
5	I like to drink tea a lot, but my younger brother prefers drinking juice.

II.

1	He grows flowers and vegetables in the garden.
2	She likes to watch basketball games, but she doesn't like to watch baseball games.
3	You can play the guitar or the piano.
4	Tom was sick, so he didn't go to school yesterday.
5	I will clean my room and do my homework tonight, but(或so) I won't go out with you.

III.

1. Besides, there are many attractions in Xinzhuang, such as Xingzhuang Temple Street, Xingzhuang Culture <u>&</u> Arts Center, <u>and</u> Xinzhuang Sports Park. (*註：& = and)

2. Among these attractions, I like Xinzhuang Sports Park most because it is very beautiful, <u>and</u> you can do many things there.

3. When I have free time, I often go there to take a walk <u>or</u> go jogging.

4. <u>And</u> if you like to watch sports games, you can watch professional baseball games in Xinzhuang Baseball Stadium, <u>and</u> basketball games in Xinzhuang Gymnasium in Xinzhuang Sports Park.

5. Many people also dance, play balls, <u>or</u> walk a dog there.

6. It is really a good place to exercise, relax <u>and</u> have lots of fun!

PART 21

副詞、
副詞比較級、
副詞最高級

重點一：副詞的功用、型態、位置

1. 副詞的功用：用來說明動詞、形容詞、句子的狀態或情形，所以是用來「修飾動詞、形容詞或整句」。

2. 副詞的型態：副詞大部分都是在形容詞後加ly而來，常見的如下：

形容詞	副詞	副詞的音標
直接在形容詞字尾加上ly		
real	really(真地)	【ˋrɪəlɪ】
great	greatly(極其)	【ˋgretlɪ】
certain	certainly(無疑地)	【ˋsɝtənlɪ】
careful	carefully(小心地)	【ˋkɛrfəlɪ】
beautiful	beautifully(美麗地)	【ˋbjutəfəlɪ】
interesting	interestingly(有趣地)	【ˋɪntrəstɪŋlɪ】
字尾是e者，去掉字尾e，而後再加ly		
true	truly(真正地)	【ˋtrulɪ】
possible	possibly(也許)	【ˋpɑsəblɪ】
comfotable	comfotably(舒服地)	【ˋkʌmfɚtəblɪ】
字尾是「子音＋y」者，則須先去掉字尾 y，而後再加ily		
easy	easily(容易地)	【ˋizɪlɪ】
happy	happily(快樂地)	【ˋhæpɪlɪ】
heavy	heavily(沈重地)	【ˋhɛvɪlɪ】
lucky	luckily(幸運地)	【ˋlʌkɪlɪ】
hungry	hungrily(飢餓地)	【ˋhʌŋgrɪlɪ】

形容詞和副詞同形		
early	early(早地)	【`ɝlɪ】
late	late(遲地)	【let】
fast	fast(快地)	【fæst】
soon	soon(很快地)	【sun】
不規則變化		
good	well(好地)	【wɛl】

3. 副詞的位置：

(1)一般動詞 + 副詞

例1：She is eating breakfast hungrily.

　　她狼吞虎嚥地吃著早餐。

　　*解析：副詞hungrily修飾動詞is eating

例2：The lady dances beautifully.

　　這位淑女舞跳得很優雅。

　　*解析：副詞beautifully修飾動詞dances

(2)副詞 + 形容詞

例1：She is really nice.

　　她人真的很好。

　　*解析：副詞really修飾形容詞nice

例2：This book is truly wonderful.

　　這本書真的很棒。

　　*解析：副詞truly修飾形容詞wonderful

(3) 副詞＋句子

例1： <u>Luckily</u> we arrived in time.

幸好我們及時抵達。

*解析：副詞luckily修飾句子we arrived in time

例2： <u>Unfortunately</u> he was late for school yesterday.

不幸地，他昨天上學遲到。

*解析：副詞unfortunately修飾句子he was late for school
yesterday

重點二：副詞比較級、副詞最高級

1. 動詞有三態：「原形動詞、過去式、過去分詞」

形容詞有三級：「原級、比較級、最高級」

副詞也有三級：「原級、比較級、最高級」

常見的如下：

副詞原級	副詞比較級 (字尾為er)	副詞最高級 (字尾為est)
hard(努力地)	harder	hardest
fast(快地)	faster	fastest
soon(很快地)	sooner	soonest
near(近地)	nearer	nearest
late(遲地)	later	latest
early(早地)	earlier	earliest

副詞原級	副詞比較級 (前面加上more)	副詞最高級 (前面加上most)
easily(容易地)	more easily	most easily
happily(快樂地)	more happily	most happily
carefully(小心地)	more carefully	most carefully
beautifully(美麗地)	more beautifully	most beautifully

不規則變化		
副詞原級	副詞比較級	副詞最高級
well(好地)	better	best
much(多地)	more	most
little(少地)	less	least
badly(壞地)	worse	worst

2. 副詞比較級的句型：

(1) 用在兩者之間做比較時

(2) A＋一般動詞＋副詞比較級＋than＋B 【A比B…】

例1：I run <u>faster</u> than you.
　　　我跑得比你快。

例2：My mother dances <u>more beautifully</u> than my father.
　　　我母親舞跳得比我父親優美。

例3：She got up <u>earlier</u> than her roommate this morning.
　　　今天早上她比室友早起。

3. 副詞最高級的句型：

(1) 用在三者以上做比較時

(2) 主詞 + 一般動詞 + (the) + 副詞最高級(+介係詞片語)

例1：Rose dances (the) <u>most beautifully</u> in our class.

蘿絲是我們班上舞跳得最優美的。

例2：I walk (the) <u>fastest</u> in my family.

我是我們家走路最快的。

例3：Sammi sings (the) <u>worst</u> of this team.

莎蜜是這一隊裡面唱得最糟的。

例4：I like English (the) <u>most</u>(或 (the) <u>best</u>).

我最喜歡英文了。

實際運用短文 ➡️ Track 028

Traditional Markets and Shopping Malls

Do you like to go to a traditional market or a shopping mall when you want to buy something? For me, if I want to shop for clothes, I prefer going to a shopping mall because clothes there may have pretty good quality. However, a traditional market usually sells very fresh meat and vegetables. So if I want to buy foodstuffs, I go to a traditional market more often. But in summer, shopping in a shopping mall may be more comfortable than in a traditional market, because a shopping mall is usually air-conditioned. Also, restaurants at a shopping center are really good places to have lunch and dinner, while traditional foods in a traditional market may attract foreign tourists the most.

傳統市場和購物中心

　　當你要買某些東西時，你會喜歡去傳統市場還是購物中心？對我來說，如果我要買衣服，我比較喜歡去購物中心因為那裡的衣服品質可能相當不錯。不過傳統市場通常販賣很新鮮的肉和蔬菜。所以如果我要買食材，我比較常去傳統市場。但是在夏天，在購物中心購物也許比在傳統市場舒服，因為購物中心通常有冷氣。而且購物中心的餐廳真的是午餐及晚餐的好地方，但是傳統市場的傳統食物可能最吸引外國的觀光客。

重點註解 ⟶ Track 028

1. traditional【trə`dɪʃən!】形容詞 傳統的
2. market【`mɑrkɪt】名詞 市場
3. shopping mall【`ʃɑpɪŋ】【mɔl】名詞片語 購物中心
4. shop【ʃɑp】動詞 購物
5. clothes【kloz】名詞 衣服
6. prefer【prɪ`fɝ】動詞 寧願，偏好（+ to V/V-ing）
7. pretty【`prɪtɪ】副詞 相當，頗
8. quality【`kwɑlətɪ】名詞 品質

英文文法 不知不覺 **學會了** 261

9. sell【sɛl】 動詞 賣，銷售

10. very【ˋvɛrɪ】 副詞 非常，很

11. fresh【frɛʃ】 形容詞 新鮮的

12. meat【mit】 名詞 肉

13. vegetable【ˋvɛdʒətəbļ】 名詞 蔬菜

14. foodstuff【ˋfud͵stʌf】 名詞 食材

15. more often【mor】【ˋɔfən】 副詞比較級 較常

16. comfortable【ˋkʌmfətəbļ】 形容詞 舒服的

17. usually【ˋjuʒʊəlɪ】 副詞 通常

18. air-conditioned【ˋɛrkən͵dɪʃənd】 形容詞 有空調的，有冷氣的

19. also【ˋɔlso】 副詞 也，而且

20. restaurant【ˋrɛstərənt】 名詞 餐廳

21. really【ˋrɪəlɪ】 副詞 真地

22. place【ples】 名詞 地方

23. lunch【lʌntʃ】 名詞 午餐

24. dinner【ˋdɪnə】 名詞 晚餐

25. while 句.

    while【hwaɪl】 對等連接詞 然而，但是(= but)

26. attract【əˋtrækt】 動詞 吸引

27. foreign【ˋfɔrɪn】 形容詞 外國的

28. tourist【ˋtʊrɪst】 名詞 觀光客

29. the most 副詞最高級 最…

練習題 ....

I. 連貫式翻譯

1. 游泳池真是夏天運動的好去處。

2. 而且我很胖，希望可以游泳減重。

3. 但是一個人去游泳相當無聊。

4. 所以我常跟朋友一起去。

5. 除了游泳，我們常在游泳池裡聊天聊得很開心。

II. 文法選擇題

1. Michael sings _____ in our class.

   (A) good   (B) the best   (C) beautiful (D) better

2. My boyfriend walks_____ than me.

   (A) fast   (B) quick   (C) faster   (D) least

3. This movie is _____ scary.

   (A) happily   (B) hungrily   (C) early   (D) truly

4. _____, he was hit by a car yesterday.

   (A) Lucky   (B) Luckily   (C) Unluck

   (D) Unluckily

5. Kelly is _____ amazing! She can dance and sing _____.

   (A) pretty/ good

   (B) rather/well

   (C) real/ beautifully

   (D) greatly/ wonderful

III. 請找出《實際運用短文 - Traditional Markets and Shopping Malls》一文中有運用到本單元教學討論的「副詞，副詞比較級，副詞最高級」之處，並將該部分劃上底線。

解答

I.

1	A swimming pool is really a good place to exercise in summer.
2	And I am very fat, so I hope to lose weight by swimming.
3	However, it is rather(或pretty) boring to swim alone.
4	So I often go to swim with my friends.
5	Besides swimming, we often chat happily with each other.

II.

1	B	2	C	3	D	4	D	5	B

III.

1. For me, if I want to shop for clothes, I prefer going to a shopping mall because clothes there may have <u>pretty</u> good quality.

2. However, a traditional market usually sells <u>very</u> fresh meat and vegetables.

3. So if I want to buy foodstuffs, I go to a traditional market <u>more often</u>.

4. But in summer, shopping in a shopping mall may be more comfortable than in a traditional market, because a shopping mall is <u>usually</u> air-conditioned.

5. Also, restaurants at a shopping center are <u>really</u> good places to have lunch and dinner, while traditional foods in a traditional market may attract foreign tourists <u>the most</u>.

英文 ENGLISH
GRAMMAR 文法
不小心就 學會了

副詞連接詞、
副詞子句

重點一

常見的副詞連接詞，如下：

1. 表條件：if(如果), unless(除非), once(一旦), so long as = as long as(只要)

2. 表時間：when(當) (其後多加非進行式的句), while(正當) (其後多加進行式的句), until(直到), since(自從), before(在⋯之前), after(在⋯之後)

3. 表原因：because(因為), since(既然), although(雖然), though(雖然)

4. 表目的：so that = in order that(以便⋯；如此一來⋯)

重點二

副詞連接詞出現的位置：

1. 句子 + 副詞連接詞 + 句子.

例1：Don't disturb Michael <u>since</u> he is studying.

既然麥克在念書就不要吵他了。

　*解析：since(副詞連接詞) 既然。(放在兩句中間)

例2：She left home <u>after</u> the typhoon left.

颱風過後她出家門。

　*解析：after(副詞連接詞) 在⋯之後。(放在兩句中間)

2. 副詞連接詞 + 句, 句.

例1：<u>When</u> I have free time, I usually play the guitar.

當我有空的時候，我經常彈奏吉他。

*解析：when(副詞連接詞)當…。(放在句首)

例2：<u>Although</u> English is difficult for me, it is very
important.

雖然英文對我來說很難，但它很重要。

*解析：although(副詞連接詞)雖然…。(放在句首)

重點三

副詞連接詞＋句子＝副詞子句

＊在副詞子句裡，要用「現在式」代替「未來式」。

例1：If it rains tomorrow, we will stay at home.

如果明天下雨，我們將待在家。

*解析：if＋句子＝副詞子句＝If it rains tomorrow，
因而雖然時間是明天，本應用未來式，但卻用現在式
rains來代替未來式。

例2：When she comes home, she will call you.

當她到家時，她會打電話給你。

*解析：when＋句子＝副詞子句＝When she comes
home，因而雖然時間指的是未來，本應用未來式，但
卻用現在式comes來代替未來式。

Track 029

When I Feel Lonely

When you feel lonely, what will you do? Will you call your friends, so you can talk to them about your feelings? Will you find something to do, so you can focus on it and forget your loneliness? As for me, I usually listen to music or play the guitar when I feel lonely. Music has a wonderful influence on me because it's just like an old friend to me. Sometimes, I go window-shopping when I feel lonely, since there are many people in a shopping mall or shopping street. I like to watch people buying and eating because it makes me feel warm inside. As long as I feel lonely, I come up with more positive thoughts so that I won't be defeated by negative emotions. If you try to do the same things as me, you may feel better next time when you feel lonely.

當我覺得寂寞時

當你覺得寂寞時,你會做什麼?你會打電話給你的朋友,這樣你就可以跟他們述說你的感覺?你會找事情來做,這樣你就可以專注在上面而忘掉寂寞?就我而言,當我感到寂寞時,我經常聽音樂或是彈吉他。音樂對我有極佳的影響,因為對我來說它就像一個老朋友。有時候當我感到寂寞時,我去逛街,

既然大賣場跟商店街有很多人。我喜歡觀看人們買東西跟吃東西，因為讓我內心感到溫暖。只要我覺得寂寞，我會產生更多正面的想法，這樣我就不會被負面情緒所擊倒。如果你試著跟我這樣做，下一次當你覺得寂寞時你也許會覺得比較好。

重點註解

Track 029

1. lonely【`lonlɪ】 形容詞 寂寞的，孤獨的
2. feeling【`filɪŋ】 名詞 感覺
3. find【faɪnd】 動詞 找到，發現
4. focus on 動詞片語 專注於… (= concentrate on)
5. forget【fə`gɛt】 動詞 忘記
6. loneliness【`lonlɪnɪs】 名詞 寂寞，孤獨
7. as for + N/V-ing 至於 (= as to + N/V ing)
8. wonderful【`wʌndəfəl】 形容詞 極好的，奇妙的
9. influence【`ɪnfluəns】 名詞 影響，作用
10. just【dʒʌst】 副詞 正好，就…
11. like【laɪk】 介係詞 像
12. go + V-ing 動詞片語 從事…
13. window-shop【`wɪndo,ʃɑp】 動詞 瀏覽商店櫥窗，逛街
14. since【sɪns】 副詞連接詞 既然，因為
15. shopping mall 名詞片語 大賣場，購物中心
16. shopping street 名詞片語 商店街

17. watch + 受詞 + V/V-ing　　watch為感官動詞，表「觀看」

18. make + 受詞 + V　讓…

19. inside【`ɪn`saɪd】 副詞 在裡面

20. as long as 副詞連接詞 只要

21. come up with 動詞片語 想出

22. more【mor】 形容詞比較級 更多的(形容詞三級：many/more/most)

23. positive【`pɑzətɪv】 形容詞 積極的，正面的

24. thought【θɔt】 名詞 想法

25. 句 + so that + 句(有助動詞)　…如此一來…

26. defeat【dɪ`fit】 動詞 擊敗

27. negative【`nɛgətɪv】 形容詞 負面的，消極的

28. emotion【ɪ`moʃən】 名詞 情緒，情感

29. the same…as　跟…一樣…

30. may【me】 助動詞 也許

31. 句 + next time(when) + 句.

　　next time(when)為副詞連接詞，表「下次…」

練習題

I. 連貫式翻譯

1. 我昨晚很早就去睡了，因為身體不舒服。

2. 但是今天早上卻很晚起床，因為沒有調鬧鐘。

3. 在我到達學校前，第一節已經上課了。

4. 雖然我不是故意遲到，仍受到老師的責備。

5. 如果老師了解我遲到的原因，也許就不會那麼生氣。

II. 文法選擇題

1. When Bill _____ back from school, I will give him the message.

   (A) will come (B) comes (C) is coming (D) coming

2. When she _____ John tonight, she will remind him of that.

   (A) will meet (B) meet (C) meets (D) is meeting

3. If she _____ to my home, I shall talk to her.

   (A) will come (B) comes (C) is coming (D) coming

4. They should not leave the building _____ the typhoon leaves.

   (A) before (B) with (C) after (D) or

5. He will be fired _____ he works hard.

   (A) or (B) if (C) unless (D) when

III. 請找出《實際運用短文 - When I Feel Lonely》一文
   中有運用到本單元教學討論的「副詞子句」之處，
   並將該部分劃上底線。

解答

I.

1	I went to bed early last night because I didn't feel well.
2	But I got up very late this morning because I didn't set the alarm.
3	Before I got to the school, the first class had been over.

英文文法秒學會了　273

4	Although/Though I didn't mean to be late, I was still blamed by the teacher.
5	If the teacher realized why I was late, he/she might not be so angry.

II.

1	B	2	C	3	B	4	A	5	C

III.

1. <u>When you feel lonely</u>, what will you do?

2. As for me, I usually listen to music or play the guitar <u>when I feel lonely</u>.

3. Music has a wonderful influence on me <u>because it's just like an old friend to me</u>.

4. Sometimes, I go window-shopping <u>when I feel lonely</u>, <u>since there are many people in a shopping mall or shopping street</u>.

5. I like to watch people buying and eating <u>because it makes me feel warm inside</u>.

6. <u>As long as I feel lonely</u>, I come up with more positive thoughts <u>so that I won't be defeated by negative emotions</u>.

7. <u>If you try to do the same things as me</u>, you may feel better <u>next time when you feel lonely</u>.

名詞子句

重點一

名詞子句的功用：名詞子句的功用跟名詞一樣，可當「主詞、受詞，或補語」。

重點二

名詞子句的結構，如下：

1. that + 完整句

   *完整句的定義：不缺主詞或受詞，如下：

   (1) S(主詞) + Vt(及物動詞) + O(受詞)

   (2) S(主詞) + Vi(不及物動詞)

   (3) S(主詞) + be動詞+ p.p.(過去分詞)

2. whether + 完整句

   whether表「是否」

3. where/when/how/why + 完整句

   where表「何地」，when表「何時」，

   how表「如何」，why表「為何」

4. what/who/whom + 不完整句

   *不完整句的定義：

   (1) 缺S(主詞)

   (2) 缺O(受詞)

   (3) 缺C(補語)

   what表「什麼」，who表「誰」，whom表「誰」(受格)

例1：The fact is <u>that he doesn't love you</u>.

事實是他不愛她。

　*解析: that he doesn't love you = 名詞子句 = that + 完整句。

　〔在這裡做補語(C)。〕

例2：He wants to know <u>whether she can lend him some money</u>.

他想知道她是否可以借錢給他。

　*解析: whether she can lend him some money = 名詞子句
　= whether + 完整句。〔在這裡做受詞(O)。〕

例3：I don't know <u>when they left</u>.

我不知道他們何時離開。

　*解析: when they left = 名詞子句 = when + 完整句。
　〔在這裡做受詞(O)。〕

例4：Can you tell me <u>where you live</u>?

可以告訴我你住在哪裡嗎?

　*解析: where you live = 名詞子句 = where + 完整句。
　〔在這裡做受詞(O)。〕

例5：This is <u>what she is looking for</u>.

這就是她正在找的東西。

　*解析: what she is looking for = 名詞子句
　= what + 不完整句。〔在這裡做補語(C)。〕

例6：The teacher wants to know <u>what is going on</u>.

這個老師想知道現在怎麼了。

　*解析: what is going on= 名詞子句 = what + 不完整句。
　〔在這裡做受詞(O)。〕

英文文法 不小心 學會了　　277

A Brokenhearted Love

Three years ago I fell in love with a beautiful girl, Kelly. courted her for one and a half months and it was so wonderfu that we became lovers soon. We loved each other so much that we were together almost every day. However, sometimes Kelly didn' know how to express her feelings and let me know what was going on. What's worse, she didn't know what she wants in her life. Although we knew that we loved each other, she still felt very upset about our future. Finally, she decided to break up with me and I felt so sad. We didin't know how we could go back to the old days, and couldn't even be friends. We are just like strangers now For me, it is really a brokenhearted love.

令人心碎的愛情

三年前我愛上了一個美麗的女孩——凱莉。我追求她一個半月，而我們很快變成了愛人，真是如此美好。我們是如此相愛，以致於我們幾乎天天在一起。然而，凱莉有時候不知道如何表達自己的感覺，以讓我知道發生什麼事。更糟糕的是，她不知道生命中想要的是什麼。雖然我們知道彼此相愛，她仍然對我們的未來感到非常不安。最後她決定跟我分手，我好傷心。我們不知道如何回到過去的日子，甚至連朋友也當不成。我們現在就像陌生人一樣。對我來說，這真是令人心碎的愛情。

1. brokenhearted【`brokən`hɑrtɪd】 形容詞 傷心的，心碎的

2. fall in love with + 人　愛上…人

   fall/fell/fallen　落下，變成

3. court【kort】 動詞 追求，向…求愛

4. half【hæf】 名詞 一半

5. lover【`lʌvə】 名詞 戀人，情侶

6. so + adj./adv. + that + 句　如此的…以致於

7. express【ɪk`sprɛs】 動詞 表達

8. feeling【`filɪŋ】 名詞 感覺

9. let + 受詞 + V　讓…

10. what was going on = what happened　怎麼了，發生什麼了

11. what's worse　更糟的是 (bad/worse/worst)

12. Although/Though + 句, 句.

    although【ɔl`ðo】(= though)　副詞連接詞 雖然

13. feel + adj.　覺得…

    upset【ʌp`sɛt】 形容詞 不安的，心煩的

14. future【`fjuʧə】 名詞 未來

15. finally【`faɪn!ɪ】(= eventually = at last = in the end)

    副詞 最後，終於

16. decide to + V (= determine to + V)　決定…

17. break up with　動詞片語 跟…人分手

18. sad【sæd】 形容詞 悲傷的

英文文法 輕鬆 學會了　　279

19. just【dʒʌst】副詞 正好，就

20. like【laɪk】介係詞 像

21. stranger【`strendʒɚ】名詞 陌生人

22. for【fɔr】介係詞 對…而言

練習題

I. 連貫式翻譯

1. 強森昨晚沒有來吉他社。

2. 我問他為什麼不來和我們一起練習吉他。

3. 他告訴我昨晚身體不太舒服。

4. 但他的好友艾琳說他並沒有說實話。

5. 事實上，我們都不知昨晚他到底發生了什麼事。

II. 文法選擇題

1. We didn't know _____ they had the face to ask for such a thing.

   (A) how   (B) what   (C) who   (D) which

2. She often does _____ without considering her friends' feelings.

   (A) what she wants to do   (B) what does she want to do

   (C) that she wants to do   (D) how to do

3. Do you know _____ is going on?

   (A) what   (B) which   (C) that   (D) how

4. Mark would never know _____ his parent's life would be like in the 1980s.

  (A) where   (B) how   (C) which   (D) what

5. Are you willing to tell me _____?

  (A) why were you absent yesterday

  (B) where do you live

  (C) when will you come

  (D) what I should do next

III. 請找出《實際運用短文 - A Brokenhearted Love》一文中有運用到本單元教學討論的「名詞子句」之處，並將該部分劃上底線。

I.

1	Johnson didn't come to the guitar club last night.
2	I asked him why he didn't come to practice the guitar with us.
3	He told me that he was not well last night.
4	But his friend Eileen said that he didn't tell the truth.
5	In fact, we all don't know what actually happened to him last night.

II.

1	A	2	A	3	A	4	D	5	D

III.

1. I courted her for one and a half months and it was so wonderful that we became lovers soon.

2. However, sometimes Kelly didn't know how to express her feelings and let me know what was going on.

3. What's worse, she didn't know what she wants in her life.

4. Although we knew that we loved each other, she still felt very upset about our future.

5. We didin't know how we could go back to the old days, and couldn't even be friends.

假設語氣

與現在事實相反的假設語氣

1. If + 主詞 + 過去式動詞/were..., 主詞 + 過去式助動詞
   (should/would/could/might) + 原形動詞

例1：If I <u>were</u> you, I <u>would buy</u> a new car.

　　如果我是你，我會買一輛新車。

　　*解析：In fact, I am not you, and I will not buy a new car.

　　事實上，我不是你，我也不會買新車。

　　→跟現在事實相反

例2：If I <u>had</u> one million dollars, I <u>could buy</u> that apartment.

　　如果我有一百萬，我可以買那棟公寓。

　　*解析：In fact, I don't have one million dollars, and I
　　can't buy that apartment.

　　事實上，我沒有一百萬，我也無法買那棟公寓。

　　→跟現在事實相反

2. But for/Without + 名詞(片語), 主詞 + 過去式助動詞
   (should/would/could/might) + 原形動詞

例1：<u>But for</u> your help, I <u>might be</u> fired.

　　如果不是你的幫忙，我也許會被解僱。

　　*解析：In fact, you help me, and I am not fired.

　　事實上，你幫我，而且我沒有被解僱。

　　→跟現在事實相反

例2：<u>Without</u> water, we <u>should die</u> in a few days.

　　沒有水的話，我們應該過幾天就活不下去了。

*解析：In fact, we have water, and we will not die in a few days.

事實上，我們有水，而且我們幾天後不會死亡。

→跟現在事實相反

重點二

與過去事實相反的假設語氣

1. If + 主詞 + had p.p...., 主詞 + 過去式助動詞 (should/ would/could/might) + have p.p.

例1：If I <u>had had</u> enough money, I <u>would have bought</u> that book last night.

如果我有足夠的錢，昨晚我就會買下那本書。

*解析：In fact, I didin't have enough money, and I didn't buy that book last night.

事實上，昨晚我沒有足夠的錢，而且也沒有買下那本書。

→跟過去事實相反

例2：If he <u>had rent</u> a car, he <u>should have gone</u> to the party last Friday.

如果他有租車，他就應該會參加上周五的派對。

*解析：In fact, he didin't rend a car, and he didn't go to the party last Friday.

事實上，上周五他沒有租車，而且也沒有參加派對。

→跟過去事實相反

英文文法私下學會了

2. But for/Without + N, S + 過去式助動詞 (should/would/could/might) + have p.p.

= If it had not been for + N, S + 過去式助動詞 (should/would/could/might) + have p.p.

例1：<u>But for</u> the heavy rain, they <u>could have had</u> a barbecue in the park last weekend.

= <u>Without</u> the heavy rain, they <u>could have had</u> a barbecue in the park last weekend.

= <u>If it had not been for</u> the heavy rain, they <u>could have had</u> a barbecue in the park last weekend.

如果不是因為大雨，他們上周末就可以在公園烤肉。

*解析：In fact, it rained heavily last weekend, so they didn't have a barbecue in the park.

事實上，上周末下了大雨，所以他們沒有在公園烤肉。

→跟過去事實相反

例2：<u>But for</u> your suggestion, I <u>should have failed</u> in the examination.

= <u>Without</u> your suggestion, I <u>should have failed</u> in the examination.

= <u>If it had not been for</u> your suggestion, I <u>should have failed</u> in the examination.

如果不是因為你的建議，我應該不會通過考試。

*解析：In fact, you gave me your suggestion, so I didn't fail in the examination.

事實上，你給了我你的建議，所以我考試沒有失敗。

→跟過去事實相反

重點三

不協調的假設句

＊If + 句(had+p.p), 句(過去式助動詞(should/would/could/
　might) + 原形動詞).

→如果當時...(與過去事實相反), 現在就...(與現在事實相反)

例1：If he <u>had made</u> a lot of money last year, he <u>would buy</u> a
　　new house now.

　　如果去年他賺很多錢，他現在就會買新房子了。

　　＊解析：In fact, he didn't make a lot of money last year,
　　so he doesn't buy a new house now.

　　事實上，去年他並沒有賺很多錢，所以他現在也沒有買新房子。

　　→一邊與「過去事實」相反，另一邊與「現在事實」相
　　反，所以是不協調的假設句。

例2：If she <u>had had</u> a better education before, she <u>could have</u>
　　a good job now.

　　如果她以前有接受較好的教育，她現在就可以有份好工作。

　　＊解析：In fact, she didn't have a better education before,
　　so she can't have a good job now.

　　事實上，她以前並沒有接受較好的教育，所以她現在也沒
　　有好的工作。

　　→一邊與「過去事實」相反，另一邊與「現在事實」相
　　反，所以是不協調的假設句。

If I Could Read People's Thoughts

If I could read people's thoughts, I would want to know what my parents think, because they always tend to keep preaching to me and it makes me upset. And it also makes me unhappy. Sometimes I even can't feel quiet when I study.

So if I could read my parent's thoughts, I could know what I should do next. In this way, I could run away first if they wanted to preach to me. Then I might feel happier, and I could study in a quiet mood. Maybe I could make progress in all subjects, and even get a high grade on many tests. I might even start to help my friends with their studying, and would feel much happier than before.

如果我可以知道人們的想法

如果我可以知道人們的想法，我會想知道我父母親在想什麼，因為他們總是很容易一直跟我說教，讓我不安。而且也讓我不快樂。有時候當我念書時，我甚至無法平靜。

所以如果我可以知道我父母親的想法，我就可以知道如何應對。如此一來，如果他們要向我說教，我可以先跑開。那麼我也許會覺得更快樂，而且可以帶著平靜的心情念書。也許我在所有科目上都能夠進步，甚至很多考試可以拿高分。我甚至也許會開始幫助我的朋友學習，而會比以前快樂多了。

1. read【rid】 動詞 讀懂，察覺
2. thought【θɔt】 名詞 思惟，想法
3. tend to + V 傾向於…
4. keep + V-ing 一直…
5. preach to + 人 向…人說教
6. make + 受詞 + adj. 讓…
7. feel + adj. 覺得…
8. quiet【`kwaɪət】 形容詞 安靜的，平靜的
9. next【`nɛkst】 副詞 接下來
10. in this way 介係詞片語 以這種方式，如此一來
11. run away 動詞片語 跑開
12. in a + adj. + mood 介係詞片語 以…心情
13. make progress 動詞片語 進步
14. subject【`sʌbdʒɪkt】 名詞 科目
15. help + 對象 + with + N/V-ing 幫助…對象…

練習題

I. 連貫式翻譯

1. 如果我有很多錢，我會辭掉工作。
2. 如果我辭掉了工作，我會出國旅行。
3. 如果我出國旅行，我會每天寫日記。

4. 如果我出國時每天寫日記，我也許就可以出書。

5. 如果我上周買了樂透，也許這些夢想就可以成真。

II.

1. If I _____ you, I would go to the party with her.

   (A)were   (B) was   (C) am   (D) will be

2. If he _____ time, he would play tennis with us.

   (A)has   (B) had   (C) had had   (D) will have

3. If my parents had had enough money, they _____ a new house last year.

   (A)will buy   (B) would buy

   (C) will have bought   (D) would have bought

4. If he had studied hard before, he _____ a graduate student now.

   (A)would have been (B) had been

   (C) would be   (D) will be

5. If you had gone to the concert last night, you _____ Richard.

   (A)would see   (B) saw

   (C) could see   (D) would have seen

III. 請找出《實際運用短文 - If I Could Read People's Thoughts》一文中有運用到本單元教學討論的「假設語氣」之處，並將該部分劃上底線。

解答

I.

1	If I had a lot of money, I would quit my job.
2	If I quit my job, I would travel abroad.
3	If I traveled abroad, I would keep a diary every day.
4	If I kept a diary every day when travelling abroad, I might be able to publish a book.
5	If I had bought lotteries last week, I might make these dreams come true.

II.

1	A	2	B	3	D	4	C	5	D

III.

1. If I could read people's thoughts, I would want to know what my parents think, because they always tend to keep preaching to me and it makes me upset.

2. So if I could read my parent's thoughts, I could know what I should do next.

3. In this way, I could run away first if they wanted to preach to me.

4. Then I might feel happier, and I could study in a quiet mood.

5. Maybe I could make progress in all subjects, and (could) even get a high grade on many tests.

6. I might even start to help my friends with their studying, and would feel much happier than before.

重點一

感官動詞的用法

1. sound/look/smell/taste/feel（感官V）+ adj.

   聽起來/看起來/聞起來/嚐起來/感到...

2. sound/look/smell/taste/feel（感官V）+ __like__（介. 像）+ N

   聽起來像是/看起來像是/聞起來像是/嚐起來像是/感到像是...

3. 感官動詞

hear/listen to/see/ watch/look at/notice/ smell/feel	+ O	+ ____ V-ing __ （部分過程，強調進行）
		+ ____ V ____ （全部過程, 強調事實）
		+ ____ p.p. ___ （表被動）

例1: The idea *sounds wonderful* to me.

   這主意對我來說聽起來很棒。

例2: His new song *sounds like* rock music.

   他的新歌聽起來像搖滾樂。

例3: Can you *hear* someone *knocking*?

   你聽到有人在敲門嗎?

例4: The boy *saw* a dog *run* by.

   這個男孩看見一隻狗跑過去。

例5: John *saw* the wounded（受傷的）policeman *taken* to a nearby hospital.

   約翰看到受傷的警察被送到附近的一家醫院。

1. Luna saw her husband _____ into the taxi last night.

   (A) to get　　(B) gets　　(C) got　　(D) get

2. I saw a bicycle _____ an old man.

   (A) hit　　(B) to hit　　(C) to hitting　(D) was hitting

3. Annie watched her kids _____ in the park.

   (A) playing　(B) to play　(C) played　　(D) to playing

4. The policeman noticed a man _____ on the ground.

   (A) to lie　　(B) lay　　(C) lying　　(D) lain

   *lie (動詞) 躺。其動詞變化為 lie/lay/lain/lying

解答

1	D	2	A	3	A	4	C

重點二

使役動詞的用法

1. let + 受詞 + V　【讓某受詞…】

   *let 【lɛt】 (動詞) 允許，讓 (三態同形：let/let/let)

例1：The landlord (房東) finally agreed (同意) to <u>let her stay</u>.

　　　最後房東終於同意讓她留下來。

例2：<u>Let me play</u> the guitar for a while.

　　　讓我彈一下吉他。

293

1. Judy hopes to keep a cat at home, but her mom doesn't let her _____ it.

   (A) to do　　(B) does　　(C) do　　(D) doing

2. My mother finally _____ me buy a new computer.

   (A) wanted　　(B) told　　(C) let　　(D) asked

   *want (想要) / tell (告訴) / ask (要求) + 受詞 + to + V

3. Let the boy _____ over there and eat with his classmates.

   (A) sitting　　(B) to sit　　(C) sit　　(D) sat

4. Mary should let her children _____ in the park more often. It's better for them.

   (A) playing　　(B) to play　　(C) play　　(D) played

解答

1	C	2	C	3	C	4	C

2.

主詞 (S) +	have make	+ 受詞 (O)	+ adj.
			+ V (表主動)
			+ p.p. (表被動)

＊使得，讓…

例1: Why don't you like to *have the window open*?

　　你為什麼不喜歡開著窗戶?

例2: Mr. Wang's jokes *made all his students laugh*.

王老師的笑話把他所有的學生都逗笑了。

例3: The cook *had his hands burned*.

這個廚師把手給燙傷了。

練習題：文法選擇

1. Some teachers like to make their students _____ all day long. But it is not good.

(A) studying　(B) study　(C) to study　(D) studies

2. Our English teacher has us _____ speaking English every day.

(A) practice　(B) to practice　(C) practicing　(D) practiced

3. The sad news made the child _____ loudly last night.

(A) cry　(B) crying　(C) cried　(D) to cry

4. That interesting song makes me _____.

(A) happy　(B) happily　(C) happiness

(D) with happiness

5. David really loves playing basketball, but he can't play it now. He had his hands _____ last week.

(A) hurt　(B) hurting　(C) hurts　(D) hurtful

*hurt (動詞)受傷，三態同形：hurt/hurt/hurt

解答

| 1 | B | 2 | A | 3 | A | 4 | A | 5 | A |

重點三

keep/leave的用法

使…保持在/處於…某狀態

keep/leave + 受詞(O) + 受詞補語(OC)

*此時的OC = adj. / V-ing(表主動) / p.p.(表被動) / 介片)

例1: The teacher *kept* the students *quiet*(安靜的).

這個老師讓學生們別作聲。

例2: Never *leave* children *alone*(獨自的) in the swimming pool.

絕對不要讓小孩獨自在游泳池。

例3: The girl *kept* her boyfriend *waiting* too long.

這個女孩讓她的男友等候太久。

例4: The noise *kept* me *annoyed*.

噪音讓我很惱怒。

*annoy【ə`nɔɪ】**動詞** 使生氣。這裡的annoyed為p.p.

做形容詞用。

例5: His talent *leaves* his teacher *in awe*.

他的天賦令他的老師敬畏。

*in awe(介係詞片語) 敬畏地

練習題：文法選擇

1. Don't leave your little kids _____ near water.

(A) play (B) playing (C) played (D) to play

2. The policeman asked her just a few questions, and then left her _____.

(A) peace　(B) tranquility　(C) in peace　(D) calm down

解答

1	B	2	C

重點四：

use的用法

1. use + 東西 + _ to _ + V 【使用東西去…】

　= 東西 + be used _ to _ + V 【東西被用來…】

　= 東西 + be used for + _ N/V-ing _

例1: The superstar *uses* this special pen *to sign*.

　= This special pen *is used to sign* by the superstar.

　= This special pen *is used for signature/signing* by the superstar.

　這個超級巨星使用這支特別的筆來簽名。

例2. We *use* this classroom *to do* the experiment.

　= This classroom *is used to do* the experiment by us.

　= This classroom *is used for the experiment/doing the experiment*.

　我們使用這間教室做實驗。

2. 人 + be/get + used to + __V-ing__ 　【某人習慣於…】

例1：I *am used to taking* the MRT to school.

　　我習慣搭捷運上學。

例2：She *gets used to exercising* after work.

　　她習慣下班後運動。

3. used to + __V__ 　【過去曾經(暗示現在不)】

例1：I *used to play* basketball on Sundays, but now I only

　　play the guitar.

　　以前每逢周日我都會打籃球，但是現在我只彈吉他。

例2：She *used to be* a teacher, but she retired last year.

　　她以前是老師，但在去年退休了。

練習題：文法選擇

1. Vicky _____ a professional basketball player, but now she
   only watches basketball games.

   (A) uses to be 　　　　(B) is used to being

   (C) used to be 　　　　(D) has been

2. I _____ alone. I don't want to have any roommates.

   (A) used to live 　　　　(B) was

   (C) am used to living 　(D) get used to live

3. This land _____ flowers.

   (A) used to plant 　　　(B) is used to planting

   (C) uses to plant 　　　(D) is used for planting

| 1 | C | 2 | C | 3 | D |

重點五

seem/appear的用法

＊S (非it) + seem/appear (vi.似乎) + to V或 (to be) adj.

= It seems/appears + that 句.

＊但是當it表示前面所提過的單數名詞時，仍可接不定詞。

例1: She *seems to know* more about her boyfriend than anyone else.

= ___ *It* ___ *seems that* she knows more about her boyfriend than anyone else.

她似乎比任何人都更了解她的男友。

例2: Mark *seems* very *satisfied* (滿意的) with the new car.

= *It seems that* Mark is very satisfied with the new car.

馬克對新車好像很滿意。

例3: He bought *the watch*. *It* seemed/appeared *to be* very cheap.

他買了這支手錶，似乎很便宜。

＊解說：It表示前面的the watch，因此後面可用to be。

練習題：文法選擇

1. Lisa's words appeared to _____ her husband. He looked so angry.

(A) offend (B) offending (C) offense (D) offended

2. They seem very _____ with the performance of the musician.

   (A) satisfing (B) satisfaction (C) satisfy (D) satisfied

3. _____ appeared that you are wrong.

   (A) They　　　(B) What　　　(C) It　　　(D) Who

解答

| 1 | A | 2 | D | 3 | C |

重點六

consider/think的用法

1. consider/think + A + (to be) + B (__N__ / __ adj. __)

   = regard/think of/view/see/take + A + __as__ + B

   (__ N __ / __adj.__)　【認為A是B】

例1: Kelly *considered herself* (to be) *unlucky*.

　　凱麗認為自己很倒霉。

例2: I *regard* her ___ *as* ___ my sister.

　　我把她當作姊妹。

2. 主被動的替換：

✽ consider/think + A + (to be) + B (__ N __ / ___ adj. __)

   = A + be + considered/thought + (to be)

   +B (__N__/__adj.__)

✱regard/think of/view/see/take + A + __as__ +

B(__N__/__adj.__)

= A + be + regarded/thought of/viewed/seen/taken + as

+B (__N__/__adj.__)

例1: I think _it_ my duty _to take care of the pets_.

= _It_ is thought (to be) my duty _to take care of the pets_.

我認為照顧這些寵物是我的職責。

(這裡的it = to take care of the pets)

例2: He _viewed_ the lady _as_ elegant.

= The lady _was viewed as_ elegant by him.

他認為這個女士是優雅的。

練習題：文法選擇

1. Miss Lin considered Tom's words _____; she wanted to

   report it to his parents.

   (A) forgive   (B) forgiveness

   (C) forgivable   (D) unforgivable

2. My husband _____ an honest man, or at least he never

   tells lies to me.

   (A) regards as   (B) is regarded as

   (C) considers   (D) is regarded

3. Vicky thinks basketball _____ her favorite sport.

   (A) x   (B) as

   (C) is   (D) being

| 1 | D | 2 | B | 3 | A |

find的用法

find + 受詞(O) + 受詞補語(OC)

*這邊的OC = N(片)/V-ing/p.p./adj./介片

例1: They will find it *an interesting book*.

他們會發現它是本有趣的書。

例2: I found the man *lying* on the ground.

我發現這個男人躺在地板上。

例3: The police found the thief *caught* by the strong man.

警方發現這個小偷被這個強壯的男人逮住。

例4: Did he find the job *boring*?

他發現這份工作無聊了嗎?

例5: When he got back, he found a letter *on his desk*.

當他回家時,他發現書桌上有封信。

練習題:文法選擇

1. Mr. Wang finds it _____ to get his ideas across in English.

(A) worried   (B) with difficulty

(C) hard   (D) easily

2. I found the dog _____ on the sofa and the cat _____ under the piano.

(A) sleep/wake (B) asleep/wake

(C) asleep/awake (D) slept/awake

*asleep【ə`slip】形容詞 睡著的

awake【ə`wek】形容詞 醒著的

解答

1	C	2	C

重點八

prefer的用法

❋ prefer to + V + rather than + V

= prefer + N/Ving + to + N/Ving

= would rather + V + than + V

【寧可⋯也不願⋯】

例1: He *prefers to* sleep *rather than* study math.

= He *prefers* sleeping *to* studying math.

= He *would rather* sleep *than* study math.

他寧可睡覺也不願讀數學。

例2: The child *prefers to* go out *rather than* stay at home.

= The child *prefers* going out *to* staying at home.

= The child *would rather* go out *than* stay at home.

這孩子寧可出去也不願待在家裡。

練習題：文法選擇

1. She prefers the modern cities _____ the quiet countryside.

  (A) than   (B) rather than   (C) as   (D) to

2. I prefer to _____ silent rather than _____ to him.

  (A) keep/talk   (B) keeping/talking

  (C) keep/talking   (D) keeping/talk

解答

| 1 | D | 2 | A |

重點九

stop/remember/forget的用法

* 不定詞表「未來動作」，而動名詞表「過去經驗」，
根據此原則，可判斷這三個動詞後面要接的是不定詞
(to + V) 抑或是動名詞 (V-ing)。

1. stop + | to V   停下來去做另一件事 (在停止時，另一動作尚未做)

       | Ving   停止做 (在停止時，該動作已做過)

例1: John stopped *to chat* with Mary.

  約翰停下來和瑪莉談話。(原來不是在和瑪莉談話)

例2: John stopped *chatting* with Mary.

  約翰停止和瑪莉談話。(原來在和瑪莉談著話)

2. remember + | to V　　記得要去做(記得尚未做的動作)

　　　　　　　　 | Ving　記得曾做過(記得已經做過的動作)

例1: She remembers *to send* the e-mail.

　　她記得要寄出這封電子郵件。(尚未寄出)

例2: She remembers *sending* the e-mail.

　　她記得已經把電子郵件寄出去了。(已經寄出了)

3. forget + | to V　　忘記要去做(忘記尚未做的動作)

　　　　　　　 | Ving　忘記曾做過(忘記曾經做過的動作)

例1: She forgets <u>to send</u> the e-mail.

　　她忘記要寄出這封電子郵件。(尚未寄出)

例2: She forgets <u>sending</u> the e-mail.

　　她忘記已經把電子郵件寄出去了。(已經寄出了)

練習題：文法選擇

1. I remember _____ the office about two hours ago.

   (A) to see her leave　　　(B) to see her to leave

   (C) to see her leaving　　　(D) seeing her leave

2. It's time for a break. Let's stop _____.

   (A) practicing　　　　　(B) practice

   (C) to practice　　　　　(D) at practicing

解答

1	D	2	A

重點十

表建議，要求，主張等動詞的用法

建議: propose, suggest, recommend, move	+	that + 句〔=主詞 + (should) + V〕 *should(助動詞)應該〔可省略，後接原形動詞〕
要求: request, require, ask, demand, order, provide(規定)		
主張: insist, urge(極力主張)		

例1: He *suggested* that the meeting *(should) be continued* after lunch.

他建議午餐後繼續開會。

例2: The manager *required* that I *(should) work* all night.

經理要求我通宵工作。

例3: My best friend *urged* that I *(should) quit* the job.

我最好的朋友力勸我辭掉那份工作。

練習題：文法選擇

1. I recommend that she _____ a lawyer.

   (A) find   (B) finds   (C) is finding   (D) has found

2. He asks that he _____ more time to complete the test.

   (A) give   (B) is given   (C) be given   (D) will be given

3. Mr. Chen moves that the store _____ for a year.

   (A) be closed   (B) closed   (C) should close   (D) closes

4. My teacher commanded that I _____ the singing class.

   (A) to take   (B) take   (C) taking   (D) took

解答

1	A	2	C	3	A	4	B

重點十一

表花費等動詞的用法

1. 事情(非it) + take(vt.需要) + 時間/抽象N

   = it + takes + 時間/抽象N + to V　　【某件事需要…】

例1: The meeting will *take* three hours.

   會議要進行三小時。

例2: It *takes* practice and time to play the guitar well.

   要彈好吉他需要練習和時間。

2. 人 + spend + 時間/金錢 + on N/(in) V-ing

【人花費時間/金錢在…】

例1: I *spent* 200 dollars *on* the book.

   我花了兩百元買下那本書。

例2: The young couple *spent* two months *touring* Europe.

   那對年輕夫婦花了兩個月時間周遊歐洲。

3. 事/物(非it) + cost + 人 + 錢 = it cost 人 + 錢 + to V

【某事/物花了某人多少錢】*cost三態同形

例1: The new house *cost* him a lot of money.

= It *cost* him a lot of money *to buy* the new house.

這棟新房子花費他很多錢。

例2: That dress *cost* her six hundred dollars

= It *cost* her six hundred dollars *to buy* that dress.

她花了六百元買那件洋裝。

練習題：文法選擇

1. It _____ a lot of time and patience to lose weight.

(A) costs (B) spends (C) takes (D) makes

2. Organizing a successful meeting _____ a lot of time and money.

(A) costs (B) spends (C) takes (D) makes

3. If you go to Taipei, you can _____ a whole night wandering(閒逛) around Shilin Night Market.

(A) cost (B) spend (C) take (D) make

解答

1	C	2	C	3	B

Track 032

Losing Weight

It seems that my husband has to lose weight. I find him not at ease when he joins in public activities. He looks diffident when he talks to new friends. Besides, it takes him a lot of efforts to put on a T-shirt and pants because he is just too fat. I remember helping him buckle his belt and button his buttons many times. And sometimes I see him slip and fall, but can't quickly pick himself up.

Our best friend Annie keeps persuading my husband to see a doctor. She also suggests that he eat more vegetables and exercise more. I consider it necessary for him to stop eating fried and sweet junk foods, too. But it takes us lots of patience and love to communicate with him. Usually he prefers to sleep and eat rather than exercise. He is used to being fat. Yet we will continue to use many terrible examples to persuade him and spend more time making him aware of the harm of losing health and confidence if he keeps a heavy weight.

減肥

我的老公似乎必須減肥。我發現他參加公開活動時不自在。當他跟新朋友說話時也顯得沒有自信。此外，他穿T

恤或是長褲時好費勁，因為他實在太胖了。我記得幫他繫上腰帶和扣上鈕扣好多次。有時候我看見他滑倒，卻無法很快自己爬起來。

我最好的朋友安妮一直勸我先生要去看醫生。她也建議他多吃蔬菜和多運動。我認為他有必要停止食用油炸及甜的垃圾食物。但跟他溝通花費我們好多耐心和愛心。通常他偏愛睡覺跟吃東西，而非運動。他已經習慣肥胖了。然而我們會繼續使用很多恐怖的例子來說服他，也會花更多時間讓他知道失去健康跟自信的危害，如果他持續肥胖的話。

重點註解 ⟶ Track 032

1. lose weight【luz】【wet】 動詞片語 減肥
2. at ease【æt】【iz】 介係詞片語 自在
3. join in + 活動 動詞片語 參加…活動
4. public【`pʌblɪk】 形容詞 公共的，公開的
5. activity【æk`tɪvətɪ】 名詞 活動
6. diffident【`dɪfədənt】 形容詞 缺乏自信的
7. besides【bɪ`saɪdz】 副詞 此外
8. effort【`ɛfət】 名詞 努力
9. put on 動詞片語 穿上
10. T-shirt【`ti,ʃɜt】 名詞 T恤

11. pants【pænts】名詞 長褲

12. too + adj. / adv.　太…

13. fat【fæt】形容詞 肥胖的

14. help + O + (to) + V　幫助…去…

15. buckle【`bʌk!】動詞 扣住

16. button【`bʌtən】名詞 鈕扣

17. time【taɪm】名詞 次

18. slip【slɪp】動詞 滑動，滑倒

19. fall【fɔl】動詞 跌倒

20. quickly【`kwɪklɪ】副詞 快速地

21. pick oneself up　動詞片語 站起來(尤指跌倒後)

22. keep + V-ing　一直…，維持…

23. persuade【pɚ`swed】+ O + to + V　說服…

24. vegetable【`vɛdʒətəb!】名詞 蔬菜

25. exercise【`ɛksɚˌsaɪz】動詞 運動

26. necessary【`nɛsəˌsɛrɪ】形容詞 必要的，必需的

27. fried【fraɪd】形容詞 油炸的

28. sweet【swit】形容詞 甜的

29. junk food　名詞片語 垃圾食物

30. patience【`peʃəns】名詞 耐心

31. communicate【kə`mjunəˌket】+ with + 人
　　動詞片語 跟…人溝通

32. continue【kən`tɪnju】動詞 繼續

33. terrible【`tɛrəb!】形容詞 可怕的，嚇人的

34. example【ɪg`zæmp!】名詞 例子，範例

35. be + aware【ə`wɛr】+ of + N/V-ing　知道的，察覺的

36. harm【hɑrm】名詞 傷害

37. health【hɛlθ】名詞 健康

38. confidence【`kɑnfədəns】名詞 自信

39. heavy【`hɛvɪ】形容詞 重的

40. weight【wet】名詞 重量，體重

練習題

請找出《實際運用短文 - Losing Weight》一文中有運用到附錄裡面「重要動詞的用法」的句子，並將該重要動詞劃上底線及做簡單的文法解析。

解答

1. It <u>seems</u> that my husband has to lose weight.
   解析: It seems/appears + that 句.　【附錄重點5】

2. I <u>find</u> him not at ease when he joins in public activities.
   解析: find + 受詞 (O) + 受詞補語 (OC)
   *這邊的OC= 介片 = not at ease　【附錄重點7】

3. He <u>looks</u> diffident when he talks to new friends.
   解析: sound/<u>look</u>/smell/taste/feel(感官V) + adj.
   *聽起來/看起來/聞起來/嚐起來/感到…
   【附錄1】

4. Besides, it <u>takes</u> him a lot of efforts to put on a T-shirt and pants because he is just too fat.

解析: it + takes + 時間/抽象N + to V （某件事需要…）

【附錄重點11】

5. I <u>remember</u> helping him buckle his belt and button his buttons many times.

解析: remember + | to V　記得要去做(記得尚未做的動作)

　　　　　　　 | Ving　記得曾做過(記得已經做過的動作)

【附錄重點9】

6. And sometimes I <u>see</u> him slip and fall, but can't quickly pick himself up.

解析：

感官動詞: hear/listen to/see/watch/look at/ notice/smell/feel	+ O	+ ___V-ing___ (部分過程，強調進行)
		+ ____V_____ (全部過程，強調事實)
		+ ____p.p.___ (表被動)

【附錄重點1】

7. She also <u>suggests</u> that he eat more vegetables and exercise more.

解析：

| 建議: propose, suggest, recommend, move | + | that + 句〔=主詞 + (should) + V〕*should(助動詞) 應該〔可省略，後接原形動詞〕 |

8. I <u>consider</u> it necessary for him to <u>stop eating</u> fried and
   sweet junk foods, too.
   解析：
   (1) consider/think + A + (to be) + B (__N__/__adj.__)
   【認為A是B】
   *這邊的A = it = for him to stop eating fried and sweet
   junk foods, too
   *這邊的B = adj. = necessary
   【附錄重點6】
   (2) stop + to V 停下來去做另一件事(在停止時，另一動作尚未做)
         + V-ing 停止做(在停止時，該動作已做過)

9. But it <u>takes</u> us lots of patience and love to communicate
   with him.
   解析: it + takes + 時間/抽象N + to V 　【某件事需要…】
   【附錄重點11】

10. Usually he <u>prefers</u> to sleep and eat rather than exercise.
    解析：prefer to + V + rather than + V 　【寧可…也不願…】
    【附錄重點8】

11. He <u>is used to</u> being fat.
    解析：人 + be/get + used to + __V-ing__ 　【某人習慣於…】
    【附錄重點4】

12. Yet we will continue to <u>use</u> many terrible examples to persuade him and <u>spend</u> more time <u>making</u> him aware of the harm of losing health and confidence if he keeps a heavy weight.

解析：

(1) use + 東西 + __to__ + V

使用東西去…【附錄重點4】

(2) 人 + spend + 時間／金錢 + on N/(in) Ving

人花時間／金錢在…【附錄重點11】

(3)

主詞 (S) +	have make	+ 受詞 (O)	+ adj.
			+ V (表主動)
			+ p.p. (表被動)

使得，讓…【附錄重點2】

國家圖書館出版品預行編目資料

英文文法不小心就學會了 / 何維綺著
-- 二版. -- 新北市：雅典文化事業有限公司, 民111.06
面；　公分. -- (全民學英文；64)
ISBN 978-626-95467-9-4(平裝)

1.CST: 英語 2.CST: 語法

805.16　　　　　　　　　　　　111004437

全民學英文系列　64

英文文法不小心就學會了

作者／何維綺
責編／張文娟
美術編輯／姚恩涵
封面設計／林鈺恆

法律顧問：方圓法律事務所／涂成樞律師

總經銷：永續圖書有限公司
永續圖書線上購物網
www.foreverbooks.com.tw

出版日／2022年06月

雅典文化

出版社
22103　新北市汐止區大同路三段194號9樓之1
TEL　(02) 8647-3663
FAX　(02) 8647-3660

英文文法不小心就學會了

雅致風靡　典藏文化

親愛的顧客您好，感謝您購買這本書。即日起，填寫讀者回函卡寄回至本公司，我們每月將抽出一百名回函讀者，寄出精美禮物並享有生日當月購書優惠！想知道更多更即時的消息，歡迎加入"永續圖書粉絲團"

您也可以選擇傳真、掃描或用本公司準備的免郵回函寄回，謝謝。

傳真電話：（02）8647-3660　　　　電子信箱：yungjiuh@ms45.hinet.net

姓名：		性別：	□男　□女
出生日期：　年　　月　　日		電話：	
學歷：		職業：	
E-mail：			
地址：□□□			
從何處購買此書：		購買金額：	元
購買本書動機：□封面 □書名 □排版 □內容 □作者 □偶然衝動			
你對本書的意見： 內容：□滿意□尚可□待改進　　編輯：□滿意□尚可□待改進 封面：□滿意□尚可□待改進　　定價：□滿意□尚可□待改進			
其他建議：			

總經銷：永續圖書有限公司

永續圖書線上購物網

www.foreverbooks.com.tw

您可以使用以下方式將回函寄回。

您的回覆，是我們進步的最大動力，謝謝。

① 使用本公司準備的免郵回函寄回。

② 傳真電話：（02）8647-3660

③ 掃描圖檔寄到電子信箱：

　　yungjiuh@ms45.hinet.net

沿此線對折後寄回，謝謝。

221-03

雅典文化事業有限公司　收

新北市汐止區大同路三段194號9樓之1

雅致風靡　典藏文化